The Testamint of Merlin

the
Testament
of
Merlin

Théophile Briant

translated from the French by

Gareth Knight

SKYLIGHT PRESS

This English translation first published in Great Britain in 2016 by
Skylight Press, 210 Brooklyn Road, Cheltenham, Glos GL51 8EA

Published with the kind permission of Éditions Honoré Champion, Ferney-
Voltaire, France.

Designed and typeset by Rebsie Fairholm
Printed and bound in Great Britain by Lightning Source, Milton Keynes

www.skylightpress.co.uk

ISBN 978-1-910098-02-8

Théophile Briant and
The Testament of Merlin

Théophile Briant needs no introduction in France, as a remarkable patron of the arts. From an old windmill and lighthouse in Brittany, (*Le Tour de Vent*), he published, between 1936 and his death in 1956, a remarkable journal (*Le Goëland*, or *The Seagull*) devoted to poetry, the arts and the esoteric. A line of interest that accords closely, as it happens, with that of Skylight Press. A great enthusiast of all things Breton and Celtic, he spent twelve years writing this evocative and powerfully esoteric novel, which was not published until nineteen years after his death and amazingly has not appeared in English until now.

Following the hints of 12th century chroniclers he places the Last Battle of Arthur and the Knights of the Round Table at Salisbury in c.548 AD, melding history and legend together. This was a time of direct confrontation between Saxon and Celt on the one hand, and Pagan and Christian on the other. From this historical scenario he follows the life and work of the founder of the Round Table fellowship, his return of Excalibur to the Lake, his safe conduct of Arthur to Avalon, his liaison with Viviane and the Faery powers in the Forest of Broceliande, and the resuscitation of his disciple Adragante in the Cauldron of Keridwen – including a remarkable sequence of initiations for the young knight. For it is Adragante who is called to bear witness to his Master's life, his death at the hands of some shepherds at Drumelzier on the Scottish borders, and his subsequent apotheosis.

Much of this is of great contemporary relevance in the current confrontation of Christian and Neo-Pagan dynamics – the Religion of Divine Love and the Religion of Ancestral Wisdom. The question being – are they so irreconcilable as is sometimes thought?

PART ONE

I

The sea was heaving gently, sending cold sword-like reflections to the far horizon. It was the summer solstice, and a great June sun turned gradually to crimson as it sank slowly over Cape Fréhel.

Some cable lengths from the shore, a powerful looking ship was swinging on its moorings. As it was being prepared to cast off, the shouts of its crew were answered by the sharp cries, like so many women, of myriad gulls beating their wings under the overhanging cliffs.

On the high prow, in the form of a seahorse, a golden sword was fixed, surmounted by a five pointed star. To starboard, along the length of the hull, eight metallic letters glistened, giving the name of the ship: CORNWALL.

It was Merlin himself, architect and master craftsman, who had presided over the assembly of planks of oak chosen from amongst the trees of the sacred woods.

An extraordinary vessel, it was thought unique on all the Celtic seas. A hundred and fifty feet long, more elegant in form than the dragon fronted ships of the Vikings, of which some remarkable specimens were already known, but the *Cornwall* seemed to have perfected the boldest innovations. Crenelated with the shields of the crew, it appeared like a fabulous serpent ever ready to attack, coiled on the deep swell and the treacherous waves.

They called it the magic boat after they had seen it plough through the sea against the wind. Besides which, no other vessel could match it for speed. And did it not fly the banner of the invincible Arthur, the son of Uter-Pendragon, and king of all the Bretons?

Leaning on the guard rail over a skiff attached to the Cornwall by a rope, a young man, almost adolescent, with fair curly hair and shining face, watched the summit of the promontory from which the light was gradually departing. He had less the air of a warrior than of a page.

A squire approached him.

"Night is falling and we're all ready. Who are we waiting for?"

"Someone without whom we can't attempt the voyage."

"Surely not the pilot?"

"No, more important than that."

"Who then?"

"Merlin, the king's bard."

"The druidess's bastard?"

The young man stepped back a pace with a menacing eye.

"I see you're new here! Who are you to speak like that about our master?"

"Ronan, the Seneschal's new squire."

"And you got that idea from him?"

"Yes … Isn't it true?"

"It's a foul lie! The Seneschal may be foster brother of our king, but he's not really one of us. And he hates Merlin."

"He doesn't hate him," replied the squire, "he just thinks he's useless."

"Useless? One who holds the secrets of the Word?"

"I don't believe that any more than my master does."

"But this ship that carries us at this moment on the waves, this new sail that's going to take us to Cornwall, perhaps you'll agree to believe in that?"

"What's that got to do with Merlin?"

"He's the designer and creator of the *Cornwall*. Better than that. It was he who had the idea to replace the square sail of the Vikings with a triangular sail to use that mysterious force they call the wind, even when it is against us."

"Impossible."

"You'll soon see for yourself."

"You seem very sure of yourself. Do you owe that to your master Merlin?

"I'm his chosen disciple."

"And what's your name?"

"Adragante the Gaël."

The squire looked at him in silence for a few moments and then continued:

"Then are you one of the Knights of the Round Table?"

"Yes," replied Adragante. "And we're all met here on our own vessel, to sail to the North and take part in our last battle."

"How many of us are there?"

"About seventy, without counting a dozen oarsmen. All the rest left yesterday with the horses of the king's guard. We'll easily catch them up before the coast of Cornwall."

"As long as we do leave," joked the squire. "The sun has almost set and when Merlin arrives – assuming he does arrive – it will already be night."

"It won't be night."

"What do you mean?"

"If Merlin chose the date of the solstice to weigh anchor, it's because it's the only night of the year when the starlight is like day. Look for the star Hesperus which will soon appear in the sky. That will be the signal."

"What signal?"

"You'll see."

At that moment a phosphorescent clarity bathed the sky and the sea, then a far shock was heard as if an anchor had been thrown into the waves.

"What was that noise?" asked the squire.

"The sun has fallen into the sea … over there, beyond Avalon, the isle of green apples. The happy island, where the sun shines that has never been seen, the sun of the Faeries."

At that moment the king arrived brusquely, came up to Adragante and clapped an iron clad fist on his shoulder. Bare headed, his silvered hair spread over his coat of mail, and the lines of his forehead were crossed by an old scar. He towered over the youth with his colossal size.

"It's time!" he said, after a pause. "Isn't Merlin here yet?"

"He's coming, I'm sure," replied Adragante.

"I hope so," continued the Breton chief. "We need to disembark at the Isle of Vecta as soon as possible. This chastisement can't wait any longer. Before the end of the month I want to have taken the battle to that cursed traitor Mordred. Have you seen any sign from Merlin?"

"I've been expecting it at sun set."

"Right. I'll give him one turn of an hour glass. For it would cost me dear to sail from Armorica without our beloved bard. I know old Klémor is with us, but although he once chanted us to victory, he is close to the land of shadows now."

At these words, an old man dressed in white came up, leaning on an ash stick and turned his dim eyes towards the king.

"Prince of Brittany," he said, "I thank you for having brought me with the army one last time. But the light has long left me, and as you well know, Merlin is the only real master of this ship."

Some knights had approached and stood in a group round Arthur.

"Only he knows how to handle the new sails," said Guinebaud, who was in charge of the rudder, a vast oar at the stern, placed on the starboard side like those of the Vikings.

"And what would happen to us," continued Adragante, "if we didn't have Merlin to chant the bard's song before the battle and lead us to victory?

"Couldn't Klémor replace him for the chant?" suggested a voice.

"No, not now," said the old bard, bowing his head. "It would need to be able to see the enemy!"

"As for me," cried Adragante, "when I hear the voice of Merlin rising before the shock of the swords, it's as if a fiery wine was being poured through my veins."

"I have no need," interrupted the Seneschal with disdain, "for a poet to come and spout drivel to help me split the skull of a Saxon dog!"

Driant de la Forest, the red headed standard bearer, who had the reputation among the knights of being strong enough to wrestle a bear, energetically rose to this raillery.

"Bravery before an enemy is nothing much. What is war, after all, but a game where skill and cunning dispute brutality? Anyway Merlin knows how to fight. He's already proved it. But each time, as you know, it was to save the life of one of the brothers of the Round Table."

A murmur arose under the shrouds.

"Merlin," approved Guivret de Lamballe, "joined our ranks to teach us another lesson than the sling shot or the axe. When I was wounded in the thigh and fallen to the ground with this Saxon about to swoop down on me, lance in hand, I swear the bard stopped him just with a look. The blow would have pinned me down in my own blood. His mysterious strength is above and beyond any of us."

"Where does it come from, this strength?" cut in the Seneschal brutally. "The lost rhapsody of dreams or the infernal gods? If you're the son of a demon it's perhaps easier to cast spells than to throw a spear like a prince of Armorica."

"Be silent!" commanded Arthur. "It was you yourself who refused to sit among us. So do not pass judgement on the founder of our order. Besides, what does the secret of his birth and his life matter? What would even his errors matter if so many of our companions owe him their lives? And if, in the hour of battle, he's as brave as you?"

"He talks in riddles and his haughtiness tires me," muttered the Seneschal.

Arthur approached close and said into his foster brother's ear, "If you want to abase yourself, you only need stick to the earth."

The Seneschal bowed his head. In the face of human authority, this pure barbarian, like several still to be found in Celtica, tolerated the Prince not because of Arthur's valour or skill with the sword, but for his innate sense of authority and intuition in combat. Of equal valour, the old warrior knew very well that what he most often carried off best was that irresistible élan – a true gift of the gods – that no experience could teach and that nine times out of ten decided the victory.

However, no one was more formidable than the Seneschal in hand to hand fighting, the only form of combat he judged worthy of a brave man, for like all the early Celts, he despised 'thrown weapons'. To kill an enemy at a distance seemed an exercise in cowardice, whereas confrontation needed courage. Yet most of all he admired Cúchulainn, the son of Lug, the lance carrying hero of Celtic epic, whose standing upright before death on the evening of the 'great Carnage' represented for him the one supreme example.

Following the example of his master, the Seneschal revelled in merciless combats and fierce exploits, which he only left in order to join his young wife Yveline-la-Blonde at his manor in the Venete country. Passionate respites that sometimes lasted several weeks during which time he endlessly rode through the forests, boot to boot with his local lords. They also hunted with the falcon from first light and it was marvellous to see the beautiful Yveline riding, carrying on her fist a bird of prey with its slate coloured plumage. Very often it was night before they returned to cross the moats along with the panting beasts and hissing of the torches. Later, when the mud of the chase had dried on their boots, trunks of trees became rivers of flame in the tall hearth chimneys, and the barley beer foamed in their cups.

Life was never without risk in the forests, lost to view, submitting to the law of the jungle, but it needed just a horn call or the appearance of a squire for the Seneschal to leave the beasts of prey, mount his war horse and resume the hunt after men or bar the way to northern pirates who landed without warning on the shores of Armorica, seeding terror along the coasts. Around this invincible centaur a certain number of Bretons gathered with ideas as simplistic as their chief, but with a complete devotion and ever ready to suppress with a rough form of justice all excesses of brigandage.

The Seneschal was thus a man of action, a body guard with no other claim but to put his sword to the service of his king.

For Arthur things were different. No doubt, like all the warlike, he had long believed in the primacy of force, and his own irrefutable judgement. But he was equally a Celt with a soul avid for the infinite, and, from his first dealings with Merlin, he glimpsed a higher law governing the apparent disorder of the world. He understood that matter was worthless in itself, and that there perhaps existed a unique and fundamental spiritual truth above earthly pleasures and the simple corporal prowess on which men of war prided themselves.

As for hired men, no doubt they were necessary for the Breton king to maintain his power, and the Seneschal was there to represent them. But it was to the bard with the golden neck torque that he owed his superior mission to orient and govern subordinate spirits. A predilection that never ceased to be remarked upon by warriors from whom Merlin kept his distance. From this arose this jealousy that expressed itself in all proposals against his person and authority.

The Seneschal regarded magic and initiation as foolishness. And if he admitted that Merlin was as brave as him in battle, the fact that he wanted to carry a lyre rather than a weapon like everyone else, was absolutely incomprehensible to him. All this resulted in the differences between the Seneschal's clan, who exclusively represented the warrior spirit, and the fraternity founded by Merlin, which already incarnated the ideal of future chivalry.

Little by little the murmurs about getting under way had ceased and a heavy silence caused by the anxiety of the crew spread to the bridge of the *Cornwall*, the silhouette of which was profiled against the old gold of the sky. The ship too seemed aware of its complete immobility on its anchors, and the sea itself seemed as if it were lying in wait, like a living creature holding its breath. The seven stars of the Great Bear shone behind the Isle of Cézembre, and the Pole Star lit its lamp at the zenith.

Driant de la Forest approached Adragante, still on the look-out, his eyes fixed on the top of the cape where the last foothills of the forest ended. He pointed to the sky. "The Chariot! The King's constellation. It's time! What is the Master doing?"

"He's coming," replied Adragante, without turning his head.

"How do you know?"

"Look over there!"

Adragante seized the wrist of the young colossus and pointed to the land before them. He laughed quietly, wide eyed, and Driant of the Forest began to laugh as well.

"Look!"

An immense flame darted its red tongue towards the Guildo, above the massif of the forest, and crept horizontally along the length of the reddened sky. Almost immediately, other flames shot up from various points along the coast, like earthly stars of fire. Distant shouting accompanied the crackling of each new brazier, and in the limpid air their smoke spread straight up, obscuring the clearness of the sky.

Everyone rushed to the starboard side at risk of capsizing the *Cornwall*.

"The Fire festival, the feast of Alban!" they cried.

"To your posts!" commanded the captain.

Arthur had gone to the prow of the ship, his hand on the hilt of his sword.

"He's going to salute the Fire, lit by the master," murmured Adragante. "He's going to draw Kaledvoulc'h from its scabbard. The magic sword. The one that only he was able to draw from the granite stone and that showed him to be the chief. Yes. The royal test! Be quiet!"

The Breton king had unsheathed and directed the point of Kaledvoulc'h at the Pole Star.

"Forgive us, Merlin," cried the king in a loud voice, "for having forgotten that this day of departure was the festival of the solstice and the sun's height. I thus salute with you our master, the pure star which on this date attains the highest point in the sky. And I salute the first sacred Fire, lit by your hands, that represents the Sun, and the Fire – immaterial Principle, from which we receive Light and Life."

The sky was now like an immense fire, and the waves now rolling to the shore seemed red as blood.

Suddenly a galloping knight surged onto the reddening desert of the crest, quickly followed by a squire, who leaped with his horse at the same time as he made a rapid half turn toward the forest. At this distance, and in the twilight, the new arrival was hardly visible, but all recognised him with a single cry.

"Merlin!"

Adragante had already leaped into a boat and seized the oars as the bard came down the gorse path that led to the creek.

A few minutes later, the Druid approaching the *Cornwall* from astern came aboard in the midst of orders for sailing, and received the greetings of Klémor and the king. He was taller than Arthur, although less broad across the shoulders and with a longer neck. Light blue eyes with keen, mobile pupils animated his shaven unwrinkled face. Only the whiteness of his hair, that he wore long under a crown of silver birch wood, showed that he had already passed the summer of his life.

At his neck shone the golden torc of the bards, and the metal star of the pentagram. His short white tunic, embroidered with silk, was held at the waist with a leather belt. He wore the blue sash.

The moment he appeared at the handrail a strong breeze rose from the south east, agitating the great triangular sail of animal skins with convulsive movements, like the body of an eel taken by the tail, and which twenty fists of mariner-knights hoisted up the vertical stalk of the mast where the royal pennant flew. Then was the turn of the jib, a short sail on the prow, the latest invention of Merlin to facilitate the twisting course of the ship. The anchor having been raised, the mass of the *Cornwall* began slowly to move, carried by the wind and cutting through the silk of the groundswell, towards the archipelago of Scissy and the high seas.

"Thanks be to the Father," said Merlin, raising his hands toward the stars, "and may Tethra grant us favourable winds, and the Pole Star, that is her luminous messenger, lead us without harm to Cornwall!"

He then took a forked hazel wand from Adragante's hands, which had been culled at the last moon before the new year, peeled off its bark, and went to place it near Maret de la Roche, who was in charge of the wide bladed steering oar, fixed to starboard at the stern of the ship.

Around the Seneschal a group of archers spoke in low voices.

"What are those fires burning along the coast?"

"The sanctuary fires to celebrate the glory of god."

"Which god?"

"The one who is hidden in the sun…"

"I saw the first flame. It came up from the Guildo and the river of ringing stones."

"Is that why we had to wait for the sorcerer?" said the Seneschal with a hint of raillery. "Odd story! Can't the king do anything until this conjuror has lit the sacred fires and strummed his lyre?"

"Yes, he's a sorcerer," said another. "He works with the korrigans."

Ronan the squire stifled a snigger.

"I would never believe all those nursery tales…"

"However," said the same man, "didn't you notice that the wind rose from the shore just as the bard set foot on the ship. It was enough to fill the sails. We left without needing the oars."

"Simple coincidence."

"Look at our sails. Have you ever seen the like? Anyway we're moving. Is that a coincidence too?"

"Why not?"

A grey headed man, who had only one eye and wore a leather apron, planted himself before the squire and held a hammer under his nose.

"On this mallet which serves me to sharpen swords, I invite you, white nose, to take my word for it. Do you know any other men of Merlin's age who have never been wounded in battle?"

"That depends on his shield."

"Exactly. He hasn't got one! And he's always in the front line."

"And what does he do there?"

"He plays the cithara."

"Is that all he knows what to do?"

"Not at all! Look more instead of mocking." And the blacksmith pointed his finger toward the prow where Merlin, under a lantern with Adragante, watched over the course of the *Cornwall*.

"What is he doing with that wand?" asked Ronan.

"He is locating the rocks, which are very many along this channel."

"Are you trying to make me laugh?"

"You won't be laughing if you go down to the land under the waters, like the last Viking and all his men who are now supping with the squid."

"Is it true, what he says?" the squire asked his master.

"I have to admit it," replied the Seneschal. Then added quickly, speaking behind his hand: "The clown has more than one trick in his bag."

Merlin turned his head toward the group, and made a sign to the pilot to veer to starboard. His eyes glittered in the shadows like two fires of St Elmo.

"Talk more quietly," muttered the smith, pushing the squire to the front. "He can hear us. And I'm always afraid when he looks at me like that."

"Then you believe it as well?"

"In what?"

"That he is the bastard..."

The smith raised his hammer as if to break the skull of the impudent youth.

"Shut up, for heaven's sake! Do you want to die?"

"To die? Why?"

"All who make that insult are cursed, and die before the waning of the moon."

"It was my master, the Seneschal who told me that yesterday. And I can't see that he's ill!"

"Take my word for it, white nose. He needs to be more careful. And you along with him!"

"You weary me with your stories," Ronan retorted briskly. "Is that how you lost an eye?"

"Perhaps. I'll tell you later. If you're still in this world."

"One more threat and I'll throw you into the sea…"

"You wouldn't be long in following me. On board, discipline is strict. Have you ever sailed before?"

"Never. I come from the country."

"Aren't you frightened?"

"I don't see what there is to be frightened about."

"You'd change your mind perhaps if you saw a siabartha."

"What's a siabartha?"

"One of those born from a root called a mandragore, who can breathe nine nights and nine days under the water, or perform levitation in the house of the Red Branch…"

"Yes, a sorcerer, like those in my country. All liars with tales of high adventure."

"What would you say then if you saw a siabartha perform the leap of a salmon, fly from a chariot over the ears of the horses and men, and stand on the point of a lance?"

"Is Merlin one of those?"

"Yes. And invulnerable like them. He is of the race of heroes who continue to fight even when their body is so wounded that the birds of the air can fly through their rib cage."

"Anyhow, he looks to be a man just like anyone else."

"I'll tell you again, watch your step," growled the smith, looking surreptitiously at Merlin, "and hold your tongue if you value your life!"

At the other end of the ship a group of knights surrounded Klémor and conversed in the clear night as the wake of the *Cornwall* lengthened into the infinite like the train of a faery cloak. Klémor had taken his cithara, and while gently caressing the strings, his blind eyes raised to the sky, he murmured:

"Manannan, god of the waves,
Ploughs with his chariot the plains of golden seaweed,
On which the speckled salmon are like leaping sheep.
He seeks the Land of Youth like us.
But Merlin leads us to the call of destiny…"

He ceased suddenly with a shiver.

"What destiny?" asked Giflet, in a whisper.

"The one the gods reserve for heroes."

"If Merlin sees into the future, does he know what threatens us?"

"Without doubt," responded the old Klémor.

"Yet he leads us there all the same. Does he have the power to turn aside the arrow of death?"

"Life is perhaps a sorrow, and death a recompense. We need to listen to Merlin. Arthur is our king, but only Merlin is our master."

"Have you known him a long time?"

"I saw him grow up in the neimheid in the time when he was secretly raised by the Druid Pontiff," replied the blind man. "Taliésin and I watched over his childhood. But one day he confounded us all with his knowledge of divination, and we realised that this marvellous child was destined to carry the torch of the wise further than us."

"However," Griflet continued, "he has taken up both lyre and sword. It is neither bard nor ovate who have to do that to follow the steps of initiation. And Merlin, after having learned the sacred poems, was sent against the Saxons who surged upon our shores like a rising sea of flames. Yet both of you have sung at the forefront of conflict."

"Yes, first in the legions of Ambrosius Aurelianus, then with the famous Uter-Pendragon who had his banners embroidered with the sign of the black dragon. It was at his court that Merlin met his son Arthur, the future king!"

"Say no more," said Gifflet."Night draws in and it is time for rest. We must not disturb the sleep of the king."

II

Arthur the brave, Arthur the Invincible! While the *Cornwall* continued its voyage under the constellations, Merlin looked on the prince who slept not far from him on the bridge, his hand resting on the hilt of his sword. On seeing the fierce warrior fallen asleep, weaker than a new born baby, the mage thought about the frailty of the human condition. That it was enough to sink into this abyss to be no more than a poor tool of destiny. Here was the conqueror, he thought, who made the Saxons tremble. And yet the errant hand of an innocent could send him back to eternity!

Merlin, who had relieved Guinebaud at the helm, recalled the tumultuous life of this king, marked from his birth with a strange fate.

King Uter-Pendragon coveted the wife of Gorloës, duke of Cornwall – Ygerne, the loveliest creature in the Isle of Britain. The castle of Gorloës was besieged by the king, but Ygerne, warned in time of the designs of Uter-Pendragon, took refuge in the manor of Tintagel. Now the same night that Gorloës perished under the blows of the besiegers,

Uter-Pendragon took himself to Tintagel, and slipping into the alcove where the beautiful Ygerne was sleeping, profited, they say, from the darkness to pass himself off as her husband, giving her a son who received at birth the name of Arthur.

Informed of her widowhood, Ygerne agreed to become the wife of her husband's murderer, but when she learned the erotic deception in which she was the innocent party, she had the young Arthur put out to be nursed by the wife of the worthy knight Auctor, where he became the foster brother of the Seneschal Keu.

At the death of Uter-Pendragon, Arthur believed himself to be the son of the Duke of Cornwall, and was proclaimed king by the High Court for having been the only one, in the course of a test, able to pull out a sword deeply buried in a stone block.

During the coronation celebrations, which took place at Carduel, in Wales, Arthur, who was married to Guenièvre, the queen of Ireland, saw the arrival of Anna, wife of King Loth of Orcanie, escorted by maids of honour and gentlemen of high degree.

The blonde beauty and sculptural figure of this princess from the North with far away eyes did not leave the young monarch unmoved, who had inherited I know not what of the lascivious and the brutal, and whose name meant literally 'monstrous bear', or 'iron hammer to break a lion's teeth.'

We have to realise that there are families in whom fate is pleased to renew the worst predicaments, such as murder combined with incest, as if certain traits attach to certain dynasties. In fact, Queen Anna was, like Arthur, a child of Uter-Pendragon, and when, the following night, the young king, perhaps taking advantage of the darkness, penetrated the bed of the wife of the king of Orkney, he did not know that he accomplished the work of the flesh with his own sister, and was far from foreseeing what fearful events would accrue to which he would fall victim.

Merlin could not avoid shuddering at the memory of that cursed night. It seemed almost inconceivable that a spasm of furtive love between two weak creatures, three parts irresponsible, could be the origin of such a train of misfortunes. He saw here the sign of a superior fate that weighs heavily on the majority of mortals, and which ruins in a striking way any pretensions to arbitrary freedom.

No crime ever comes singly. That seems to be the law. Spilt blood is the carrier of innumerable seeds in the equivalent acts of love and murder. A crime is nothing other than a breeding of larvae that call to each other, reproduce each other and infinitely multiply.

And so Merlin dreamed of Mordred, the incestuous son of that night at Carduel. Was he not predestined by his sad birth to all the baseness and felonies, the last of which revealed him surely as a monster. It was in vain that the king, his father, told by the magus of his terrible error, had charged him to watch over the education of the young prince. Mordred was inhuman in every sense of the word. With a surly and underhand nature he responded to kindness with cynicism and to authority with deceit.

However, he grew up at the king's court among the royal ladies over whom he exercised a strange fascination, for by one of those contradictions that are customary in nature, Mordred had the good looks of a young animal, and when he leapt on his horse his body had the lithe grace of a panther.

At twenty years of age, Mordred had learned only one thing: the profession of arms, at which he was a past master. Detested by all the servants at the palace, whom he frightened by his behaviour, he nourished two deep hatreds in his evil heart. First for Merlin, whom he detested since the day the bard, having surprised him in the forest about to blind a favourite greyhound puppy of the king, had forced him to grovel before him by the sheer power of his gaze. Then for his father, whom he considered his mortal enemy, not simply because he was his son, but because he had conceived a diabolical plan to rob him at the same time not only of his crown but of his wife, Queen Guenièvre, the most beautiful of all the ladies in Armorica.

The drama came to a head during the last expedition of King Arthur to the Welsh hills. For a long time the felon Mordred had assured himself of the support of the leading Saxon chiefs, who were only too happy to have the son of their most dangerous adversary as an ally. The traitor profited from the king's absence by abducting the queen and seeking refuge with her on the Isle of Vecta, near the Saxon King Kenric. He had spent part of Spring raising an army to attack his father and had sworn to challenge him to single combat and kill him with his own hand.

During this time, Arthur, wracked with humiliation by the double treachery of Mordred, had returned to Armorica to assemble the flower of his knights and pursue the criminal son who must be hunted down and slaughtered like a wild beast.

"It is a struggle of God against the devil, and God cannot be other than with us," proclaimed the king in deciding the urgency of this expedition. "For the eternal wisdom says that the eye of a son turned against his father will be torn out by the crows of the valley."

And that was why the *Cornwall*, preceded by three other vessels, had set off for the North in full sail under a star spangled sky.

"And so," thought Merlin, "all that happens today is the consequence of a sexual dalliance between brother and sister who received the same cursed seed from their father Uter-Pendragon. And it is for me, a man of love and forgiveness, to have the cruel duty to guide this ship, driven by the winds of vengeance, toward the shores of Death!"

Through the shrouds the magus looked up to the stars, seeking for some hope there perhaps to avert the inevitable. Then he felt astonished at his moment of weakness. The constellation of Cancer reigned in the firmament, accompanied by squares and oppositions that cursed with too much evidence the transit of the king and his companions in arms. Mars in the eighth house, badly aspected with the Moon, announced a violent death. Apart from the eclipse of the Sun he had observed in the preceding year, that confirmed this prediction, and the comet he had seen two nights before in the constellation of the Charioteer between the Goat and the Twins, that also announced disaster. Born under the zodiacal sign of Scorpio, Arthur must succumb, bitten by the serpent warmed at his breast, and disappearing from this world at the hour when the nebula of the Stable appeared in the sky.

All this Merlin already knew, having read it in the left hand of the king, where the line of life was broken at the base of the Mount of Venus, indicating that he would hardly survive the third moon. And all the hands of the knights who slept at this moment on the bridge and in the hold of the ship, showed the same signs. All, except that of Lucain and of Gifflet de Fougères. And that of Adragante, who seemed reserved for a much stranger destiny.

But Driant de la Forest and Maret de la Roche and the others? Was this to be their last journey?

"Ah! To know," murmured Merlin, while skirting the crest of a reef, "to be able to see the blows of fate and be unable to do anything about them! One can no more go back to change the past than this vessel could go back through its wake, and the future for me is to lose my powers. All is ordained. All must come to pass. And my inward knowledge of all these events obliges me to obedience and to silence. I am at this moment simply a conveyer of shadows, and these sleepers, without knowing it, crossing an arm of sea of the Beyond.

"But what does it matter? This sacrificial cargo is but an instant in the world, a passing flash in the eternal voyage of souls. All these passengers who rely on me, like lost children, have come to the end of their human journey. And for the great voyage, I have given them the last rites which will allow them to go as far as the threshold of a new birth…

"Spirit is the only reality. Matter only the expression of a day, a form that moves and fades away. Creation is eternal and continues – like life. Man is a mirror of God."

The dawn lightened the mainland face of the hills, and they began to see the first isles as Gifflet de Fougères came to take the helm. A marvellous freshness ran over the somnolent sea, where foam coloured seagulls flew. One by one the stars melted from the sky.

Arthur arose in an instant, like a barbarian ever ready for combat, and Merlin, being close by him, gently touched his right hand and cheek. Then, having asked for a little fresh water for his ablutions, the bard leaned on the rail and looked long at the disappearance of the Morning Star on the horizon.

III

At the other end of the *Cornwall* the squires, artisans and men at arms slept in a circle around the Seneschal. Some of them had taken off their coats of mail or their breastplates, and their naked torsos, as they breathed, seemed to accompany the rhythm of the sea. A Saxon deserter who had taken service in the army of the Breton king had a tattoo that ran from his throat down his spinal column, representing an eel with stag's horns.

The blacksmith was heating swords. Near him, a man wearing a strange cap, his chin ornamented with a black beard with two points, was cutting out a piece of cloth with large scissors, to bind a dressing round the arm of a sailor who had been injured.

But the unguents were not enough, and the blood poured over his hands.

"Who's that?" Ronan asked his master.

"The ship's doctor."

"Can he prevent death?"

"Sometimes."

"Is he a sorcerer?"

"Not in Merlin's fashion. He boils up seaweed in pots and sews up the worst wounds with a needle. He can treat men during battle."

However, the blood still continued to flow and the injured man could be seen to be growing more pale. The blacksmith offered his red hot iron to the doctor, at the sight of which the sailor gave a great cry and fainted.

The blacksmith insisted. "There's nothing like fire to staunch a wound. The healer of the gods used it."

"The gods," said Ronan, "don't need to be cured…"

"Haven't you heard of the battle of Mag Tured?"

"No."

"I'll tell you later. But now it's a question of curing this man if we don't want him to go off in the ship of Samahan."

And he brandished the hot iron again as Merlin pushed into the middle of the group to lean over the unconscious man.

"Bring a cauldron," he told the doctor, "and take off the bandage."

The squires made a ring round him as Merlin extended his two hands over the wound.

The blood appeared to coagulate. Merlin put his hands nearer, brushing the wound with his finger tips. Two long white hands, almost immaterial, the fingers of which, some said, shone in the shadows.

"Fill the cauldron with sea water," he told the blacksmith, who had abandoned his red hot iron.

He plunged his hands into it, then put them gently on the wound, murmuring in a low voice.

"Adragante!" he called.

The young man appeared. Merlin said a few words to him and a few moments later his disciple returned with a laminated ribbon of dried seaweed that he dipped into the salt water to restore its original freshness.

Merlin cut the end and tendered it to the ship's doctor.

"Put this on the wound and replace the bandage. It won't be there tomorrow."

The mage retired, accompanied by Adragante.

An archer with a horn came to blow reveille and the men of the crew gathered round the doctor before going to their posts.

"The wound will be infected," complained the latter while applying the weed to the wound. "He should have boiled it or else used my unguents."

"Then why did you obey him?" asked the Seneschal brutally. "You've been engaged to follow your calling, not the orders of makers of charms."

"Don't forget he staunched the wound," remarked the blacksmith.

"How?"

"By waving his hands."

"You don't mean to tell me he has the power to stop blood!"

"Anyway the blood congealed… we all here saw it."

"I don't like sorcerers."

"He belongs to the race of the Filid. He has power over us."

"You are joking I trust?"

"He can put a leprosy on your face. He can curse a harvest. The Filid are the poet magicians. Their words become acts."

"You're free to lend your ears to that fine talker. As for me, I only need one word, and it's this!"

He slapped the golden pommel of his sword, and marched off towards the prow that gently cut the waves.

Ronan the squire stayed near the blacksmith and the doctor, looking curiously at the wounded man who had ceased to moan and was sleeping peacefully.

"Do you think he will get better?" he asked the doctor.

"I don't know."

The smith intervened fiercely.

"You lie! You know perfectly well this isn't the first time the Master has given you a lesson by taking a patient out of your hands you didn't know how to cure."

"Like you, with your red hot iron!"

"Shut up, scorpion!"

"Eye of a Fomor!"

At this insult the one-eyed man seized a hammer and threw it at the doctor. They had to disarm him. He spat three times over the side, the side the sun was rising, then returned to his forge, muttering to himself. But a few moments later, as the doctor turned his back to look out over the side, he seized a dagger and struck it with all his might into the centre of the man's shadow on the deck. He sniggered as the doctor gave a stifled cry.

"By water and by fire, by the Fomors who scatter the bones of the living, be cursed!" he shouted.

Adragante rushed up and quickly pulled out the dagger.

"Have you lost your head?" he said to the smith, with blazing eyes. "Here we are on the verge of battle and you throw a spell on our doctor. Who will apply the bandages? Who will cure the sick?"

The smith bowed his head.

"Was it so dangerous, what he did?" Ronan asked Adragante.

"More than you think," said the young man quietly.

"Can't your Master do anything about it?"

"If it pleases heaven!" And he added, shivering, "There is no spell more terrible than the one they call the nailing of the shadow."

Towards midday the wind fell. The masts creaked under the fluttering sails, and the *Cornwall* advanced only with difficulty under a torrid blue sky. To starboard they could still see in the solar scintillation the confused and distant mass of the forests of Armorica.

"One day" said Merlin, addressing the king, who was opening clams with a dagger, "part of this kingdom will disappear forever. Under irresistible columns of foam the cliffs on the shore will crumble to powder, and when calm returns, many of these islands, daughters of the sea, will have returned to the deep."

"If what you say is true," replied Arthur, "what is the good of people and building houses to shelter them if we and our works are the prey of some insatiable divinity?"

"We are generally the prey of someone, even a best friend," replied Merlin, swallowing a clam and showing him the empty shell. "The law of the world, for those like you who have followed the way of the flesh, is ever to create victims, and then call new beings into the circle of pain that the wise know under the name of Abred. A man who procreates – for most of the time in the blindness of pleasure – is a catcher of souls."

"Then who can resist the erosion of Time?"

"Only one thing, as you know. The spiritual Temple that we build in the beyond. That alone will survive from this world that, like ourselves, was born, and whose time will pass like ours. All of which ends shortly. But we are images of the Father of all things, and our souls belong to the infinite."

After a silence Arthur replied, "Will that be to punish the same crimes as those of the town of Ys, when the sea swallows these lands?"

No. That occasion was only a struggle of the occult forces of nature and the victory of one element over the other. Innocent victims will perish. For that is the way of the world, as in the secret rites of religions that sacrifice the innocent for the mysterious balancing of things. You forget that that law of the redemption of evil is one of the fundamentals of our belief…"

"But in the drowning of the town of Ys, you wouldn't deny that innocents equally perished?"

"Yes, but that was by the intervention of an evil will, a purely human will, at odds with destiny. In a lament that I recently composed, I sought to show the symbolic character of that catastrophe."

Adragante the Gaël heard these last words.

"Master," he said, approaching Merlin, "the pilot has no need of you.

The winds have almost dropped and the route to the North is free. Would you care to sing that poem?"

"Very well, for you," replied Merlin.

And he added as he turned toward Arthur, "For you and our beloved king, who wishes to defend the invisible Father! Go and fetch my harp and ask the old bard Klémor to come."

In the code of the Breton king Hoël it was written: 'three things cannot be beaten: the Book, the Harp and the Sword.' A sacred triad, that represented knowledge, the word of the elect (whether musician or poet), and force at the service of justice.

In the entourage of the bard they believed that a magic virtue was attached to his harp, like the sword of the king, and that in the strings mysteriously resided the gifts of courage and inspiration. Much later one saw the clans, for the same reasons, fight over the harp of a bard, in the hope that its possession would be a means of assuring victory. Only '*the force of the Art*' brought about the submission of an adversary, and through appropriate incantations, assured the alliance of the gods. Such was, in those primitive times, the supremacy of the poet, the possessor of the Word, who linked the earthly to the sacred, and kept a privilege of constraint over these powerful principles.

In the course of these functions the rhythmical cursing by a bard had to be avoided at all costs. The fact of being 'satirised' by one of them could deprive one of honour or life, and the hero of celtic cosmogonies, who was the guardian of his people, was thought to obey the 'incantations' of an adverse poet, and even, eventually, accept his ruling.

The lyre of Merlin, that was kept in a cover of crimson silk, was thus a 'talisman' that only the fingers of the initiate could touch, and Adragante, on bended knee, passed the instrument to his Master. Klémor, brought by a squire, was also seated, cithara in hand, before Merlin and King Arthur.

Merlin lifted his harp into the rays of the sun, and began by brushing the strings very lightly, while the companions on the ship, summoned by Adragante, came to sit in a circle around the singers. It was Klémor who began.

On the orders of Dahut, King Gradlon's daughter
The town of a thousand turrets was built
With casements of light, and doorways of dream
The beautiful city of Ys
By a great lock saved from the sea.

Now on one night of furious rutting
The evil Dahut, spurred by a demon
Stole the key of the lock from her sleeping father
And the two of them sneaked down to the dyke
Where her demon lover took the lock key
And opened the gates to the sea.

Then Merlin continued at a faster pace:

The Ocean, she cried, awaking her father
The Ocean has broken the gates of bronze
And with all its desire it rises toward me
Let us ride off together on Morvark your horse!
But Saint Guénolé arose and cried out to the King
Throw back the evil daughter who holds you
Or you as well will be clutched by the sea!

Then Klémor replied in his turn:

And Gradlon obeyed, and threw off his daughter
And the Ocean calmed and ceased to pursue
He spurred on his horse without looking behind him
Not daring to look back at the demon or town
Clutched by the swell, embraced by the foam
Forever lost in the depths of the sea.

And Merlin, having plucked his lyre more loudly raised his voice to finish the poem:

The Lovers now lie in a coffin of sand
In the depths of a palace haunted by eels
Dahut the Malefic there in the midst of it
Her tongue and her breasts now nibbled by crabs
Her eye sockets both as empty as shells
And her heart changed into a spider crab!

May Ys the Great continue to sleep there
In the emerald realm where the jellyfish grow
May Ys the Great sleep, along with the maiden
Disappeared by the act of a demon,
For ever submerged in the depths of the sea!

That same evening, after the king and Merlin had retired under their tent of leather and bearskin that the servants had erected to starboard under the mizzen yard, some men at arms stayed up, seated around the blacksmith, who was entertaining the sailors of the *Cornwall* with stories to break the monotony of life on board. Although the June night was clear and starlit, one could only just distinguish a confused circle of human shadows but the words cut through the silence hardly troubled by the sound of the waves against the hull of the ship.

The one-eyed story teller began, while polishing a sword:

"In olden days things were not like they are now. Men and the gods knew each other. Men spoke with the gods, and knew their language. Animals also spoke, even the fish. I'm telling you the honest truth.

"In olden days objects chose their owner. They were good servants to him, but not for others. One day, during the famous battle of Mag Tured, Ogma found the sword of Tethra, king of the Fomorians. Ogma drew the sword and cleaned it. Then the sword told her all that she had done since her birth. That was what swords did, when someone took it from its scabbard."

The blacksmith showed the sword, whose steel shone in the night.

"Today this sword is dumb. But I know its history."

"How can you know it?" asked Ronan, the Seneschal's squire.

"It speaks to me when I'm sleeping. It's a very old sword that I keep in reserve on the orders of Merlin, the bard with the golden neck torque."

"Keep it for who?"

"That's a secret."

"Can't you at least tell us where the sword comes from?"

"It took part in the battle of Mag Tured."

Voices were raised…

"Tell us! Tell us about the battle of Mag Tured!"

Then, having taken his time, the one-eyed man began:

"Actually there were two battles. In olden days the race of Partholon landed in the North, on the Isle of Mists. Partholon was the first worker. He cleared the land and the forest, and made seven lakes appear from the earth. It was Bréa who built the first house and made the first cauldron, and Malaliach who invented fern beer. This was also the time of the first adultery and the first duel. Then Malaliach introduced the Nemed and sacrifice to the gods.

"After the first duel, men imagined fighting together. Thus was the first battle set up: the race of Partholon against the Fomorians. The Fomorians were demons from under the earth who drove up like thistles and couch grass, and fought with a single foot, a single hand and a single eye. They were beaten after seven days but came back later to take on another race. It was then that the Fir Bolg appeared. They invented royalty and the iron spear.

"As peoples are never at rest, new invaders came, the Tuatha, the tribe of the goddess Dana. That was the first battle of Mag Tured…"

The blacksmith stopped to take a swig of 'gwen-ardent' from his flask.

"And who won this first battle?" someone asked.

"The Tuatha. They were the victors, although it was less by arms than by magic…"

"More old wives' tales!" laughed Ronan.

"If you keep interrupting and mocking I won't go on!"

Furious cries arose. The audience protested, wanting to know more. And Ronan, threatened with being roughly handled, promised to keep quiet.

"Very well," continued the story teller. "But no more interruptions! Only questions are allowed. I was saying that with the Tuatha, the men of art knew magic. They were of the race of gods. The workers weren't gods."

"Where did the magic come from?"

"From the possession of five talismans."

The one-eyed man paused for a few moments to increase his effect. All listened to him in a religious silence.

"Like so, five talismans. As many as the fingers on my hand."

He raised his hand to form shadows with five fingers spread.

"The first talisman was that of the thumb. It was a marvellous Cup, the Cup of the Secret. It's forbidden for anyone to say anything about it, except that it contained a magic liquid and tested the tongue of the drinker… a lie would cause it to break.

"The second talisman – that of the index finger – was the Stone of Fal that recognised a future king, and cried out when he put his foot on it.

"The third talisman, that of Saturn: the sword of Nuada, with wounds that couldn't be healed, that lit up the night like a torch, and which isn't far from here…

"The fourth talisman, that of the Sun, was the lance of Lugh that never missed its target, and returned after the blow to the fist of the lancer. That lance belonged to Cúchulainn. It was terrible when the fury took it. It poisoned its victim. It foretold the future…"

The one-eyed man stopped.

"And the fifth?" asked several voices.

"The fifth talisman," continued the smith, "was that of the little finger; the cauldron of the Dagda, the cauldron of abundance. Its contents preserved from death."

"Do they know what was in the cauldron?"

"That's a secret… but none left it without being re…" An admiring murmur drowned his words.

The smith continued:

"Those who possessed these talismans, the Tuatha, reigned over the kingdom of mists. When the Fomorians returned from the underground country, they took up arms again and declared war on them. Before the battle the chiefs met the Men of the Art. The talismans were consulted and the lance of Lugh announced victory.

"The Macha with red hair and the Morrigan promised their help. They swore to deprive the enemy chief of his heart's blood and to gnaw into his courage, and to coil themselves, in the form of needles, around the legs of his soldiers.

"The magicians, the singers and the druids made an oath to dry up the water from the lakes and springs, to rain three deluges of fire upon the Fomorians, retain the urine in the bladders of the men and horses and rot the blood of the wounded.

"The battle was terrible and lasted right through the last quarter of the moon. On one side the Fomorians, with faces the colour of ashes; on the other the Tuatha, with blue eyes, sons of the Sun.

"During the combat the royal bard chanted incantations near the magic wells where the doctor Diancecht stood. As soon as a Tuatha warrior was struck dead, they took him to the wells. The doctor plunged them into the water and they came out healed and ready to fight.

"On the evening of the seventh day, when the new moon rose, the Fomorians abandoned the field of battle and returned to the Shadows in the country of the deep. That, according to the story tellers, was the second battle of Mag Tured."

Great applause broke out. Some beat on their shields with the palms of their hands.

"It's too easy," mocked Ronan, "to raise the dead to win a battle. The game was rigged. They cheated with a spell."

"Magic isn't trickery, it comes to us from the gods," replied the blacksmith. "Diaoul also has these powers."

"And is he stronger than the gods?" asked an archer.

"That's the way things are," said the blacksmith sententiously.

"Then the gods aren't the masters?"

"Yes, just the same. Take my word for it."

"Anyway, was Cúchulainn dead?"

"Yes, he was dead… but only in appearance."

Cries went up: "Lies! How did he die? Tell us about the death of Cúchulainn!"

The one-eyed man imposed silence. For a few seconds one could hear the rippling of the sea along the length of the hull. The clearness of the night was such that the faintly silvered horizon could be seen.

"First I have to say," began the blacksmith, "that the hero whose story I'm going to tell you about died when he was born. He had no name yet but his mother Dechtire, who knew that her body had carried a hero, lay down that evening in tears. Now during the night she saw an unknown stranger approaching, who covered her with his shadow and said: 'I am the god Lugh. The son I give you will be the same as he who has just died. And he will die a second time, under the pressure of scandal, to finally merit living under his first name,which will be Sétanta, that is to say, he who was thrice born. In memory of the holy Triad.' "

"That can't be the same," interrupted a veteran.

"Yes, it was very much the same. I tell you the exact truth. Listen to what happened. Up to the age of seven Sétanta was brought up by the poet Amairgin. Fergus taught him hockey and the profession of arms, and the Druid Cathbad the arts of the gods and the secrets of magic."

"When did he become Cúchulainn?"

"Wait a little, and follow my story. Sétanta, having grown, was always the victor in combat. His hockey stick was invincible. Even his elders couldn't match him. It was then he had to match himself against the phantoms. One evening, on the battlefield, he met a half-monster who threw on his shoulders half the body of a man. He tried to defend himself with his hockey stick but was struck down. Then a voice rose from among the bodies. It said 'Bad apprentice hero, to fall at the feet of a phantom!'

"Sétanta recognised the voice of the Babd, the Celtic godmother. He got up, knocked off the monster's head with a blow of his hockey stick and went off, rolling it like a ball across the battlefield.

"Listen now to the story of Culann's fierce dog. Culann was a blacksmith like me; he had a famous dog, wicked as a bear and as big as a horse, that guarded alone the nine herds of his master. It took no less than nine men to hold its lead. Right. One evening there was a banquet at Ulster and the smith had let go his dog for the night. Now, imagine Sétanta, who was late for the banquet, arriving to find himself face to face with this ferocious beast."

"But wasn't he too young, Sétanta?" they asked.

"He was no longer a child, but was still growing. And at his age, I swear, he could be forgiven for being afraid of Culann's dog. So he called for help. But no one dare come out to defend him. What could he do before this monster whose barking shattered the night? "

"Was he armed?"

"Nothing but his hockey stick and a ball. He was little more than a child as I said. Well, when the ferocious beast threw itself at him he struck his ball into its throat so hard that it tore out its entrails. You'd think that everyone would applaud that exploit – apart for the smith who lamented the loss of his guardian. But that didn't matter! Sétanta made an oath to replace Culann's dog from now on, to protect him, not only him and his flocks but the whole of the plain of Muirthemne. 'I accept,' says the smith. 'But you must now call yourself the dog of Culann!' "

The story teller took some time to introduce this character.

"And it was thus that the young hero received his proper name, his man's name, Cúchulainn. At a single stroke he became protector of the lands of Ulster and all the goods of the people."

"And then?" asked his listeners all at once, on the way to a sleepless night.

"Then Cúchulainn received the equipment of a warrior. One after another he broke fifteen outfits until he had obtained the arms of King Conchobar. It all happened like this. He challenged in single combat the three sons of Nechta Scène who had exterminated the Ulates; he cut off their heads and retook the way of Emain Macha. He tamed two swans with a slingshot, captured a stag that he subdued with a single look, and hitched it to his chariot where the three bloodied heads of his enemies rolled. He came, in this fashion, before the ramparts of the town from whence Queen Mugain had sent naked women to test him. Thus he acheived the status of a man and the queen dressed him in the manly toga. How handsome he was, this Cúchulainn! He was a giant. His three coloured hair was adorned with a hundred chains of carbuncles; a hundred torques of red gold shone on his chest. He had seven pupils to his eyes and seven fingers and he juggled before his people with seven heads."

"I don't believe any of this!" exclaimed Ronan.

"That's up to you," retorted the smith. "You can't compare your puny skin with a hero like Cúchulainn, who carried on him, in his person, all the sacred numbers! He was an astraïde and a siabartha. He could do all these amazing feats or invented them! He crossed a hall ninety-five feet wide on a tightrope. He could become as tall as the highest tree in the forest! No one could ever be healed of his wounds!"

"Then how do you explain," asked a pilot, "that a hero that strong could lose his life?"

"By treason. By plot and black magic. And that was the Great Slaughter of Mag Muirthemne."

"Tell us about the Great Slaughter."

"I should tell you that Cúchulainn, whom all the girls of Ulster loved, had been looking for a wife at first at the house of Scathatch of the Shadows, where he unhinged the door with the butt of his lance. Then in the triple fortress of Forgall, where he conquered Emer by abduction after having accomplished the thunder feat that killed three hundred and nine men! It was already a long time since he had cut the throat of Calatin le Hardi and his twenty-seven sons. But the wife of this last, whom he had spared, brought three sons and three daughters posthumously into the world in a single birth. Queen Mebd, charged with the vengeance of the clan, decided to make sorcerers of all this brood. In the end, she had the right foot and left hand of each of the boys cut off, and the daughters had their left eye put out. They had to give up this eye to discover secrets, so the mutilation was necessary. The same as when the dead were brought back to life in the Magic Cauldron, they were dumb."

"Well," said the Seneschal's squire, "you might have lost your right eye, like the sorcerers. But in the devil's name you've not lost the use of your tongue!"

The smith picked up a horse shoe and leaped up before him:

"Ginger cat! Cursed toad! May your blood rot at the next moon!"

They held him back to prevent him throwing the horse shoe at Ronan's head. The Seneschal had approached to demand silence as it was the middle of the night, besides which they had to change the men of the watch, and each went to his post grumbling about not hearing the end of the death of the hero Cúchulainn.

Two were over-excited enough to approach the smith and ask him for the end of the story. The one-eyed man refused at first, but the Seneschal himself came to sit nearby, wanting to know the rest of an epic that had stirred the blood of his rough soldiers.

"For seventeen years," continued the smith, "the children of Calatin wandered the world, learning magic. For seventeen years they forged magic spears to serve their vengeance. When all was ready Queen

Mebd met the warriors of the North and the Great Slaughter began. But Cúchulainn, the great Guard Dog of the land of Ulster was up to then invincible. Invincible on condition that he never killed or ate a dog, for he knew from the crow goddess that his first and last exploit would be the death of a dog, and that all magic would turn against him.

"But having left for the combat, the hero met the three daughters of Calatin, who were roasting a dog over a branch of rowan, chanting incantations. Now the hero was prey to a 'geis' – the geis of his lineage, the geis of his clan – that obliged him never to pass before a hearth without tasting the food that was offered him. Whilst his other geis forbade him to eat dog – what could he do?"

"What did he do?" demanded the Seneschal.

"He took the shoulder of the dog that the sorceresses offered him, placed it under his left thigh and remounted his horse, the Grey of Macha – and quickly realised he was lost."

"How?"

"Because his hand and thigh withered. He had ceased to be invincible."

"What happened in the end?"

"On the field of battle, a Filid demanded his lance, threatening, if he refused, to take away his honour – that's the law, as you know. Cúchulainn threw his lance but in such a way that it transfixed the poet and nine men with him."

"Hurrah!" cried the Seneschal.

"Lugaid, the greatest enemy of Cúchulainn, then seized the first magic lance, forged by the sons of Calatin, and threw it at the hero. Cúchulainn parried the blow and tore the lance from the mortally wounded body of his neighbour, so as to be armed again. As they threatened to satirise the people of Ulster, of which he was the chief protector, he abandoned a second and then a third lance, for the honour of his race."

"So then he's disarmed?"

"Yes. And done to death by the lance of Lugaid. That was the end. His entrails spilled out into his chariot."

"Was he dead?"

"No, not yet. He asked his adversaries to let him drink from the lake, which they let him do. Gathering up his entrails, he went down to the bank, drank the fresh water and bathed his terrible wounds. But a dog came to lap the water reddened by his blood. So Cúchulainn killed it with a sling shot. Bad luck. Thrice bad luck. The death of the dog is the prediction of the Babd, it is the accomplishment of his destiny! There is nothing more for the hero to do but face the pack of his enemies, waiting for his eye to be closed with the opaqueness of death. He tied himself with his belt to a standing stone so as to die standing before it, while his horse, the Grey of Macha, to protect him in his agony, killed fifty men with its teeth and hooves. But the moon of the hero goes out on Cúchulainn's forehead, his sight darkens, and a crow comes to perch on his shoulder.

"He's dead. Lugaid dares to approach him to cut off his head but the sword that fell from the hand of the Invincible gave a savage cry and cut off the Lugaid's right hand.

"Oh sacred head, resting on the stone! Your warmth splits the granite at the moment that Conall, the brother of Cúchulainn, pursues Lugaid and brings back a garland of enemy heads threaded on a wicker strand! He is avenged, the great Guard Dog of the land of Ulster! May his wife arrive, dishevelled, shedding tears of blood! May his wife, Emer of Forgall, lie on his body for the last espousals! She has to do no more than put her lips to those of the cut off head. She has to do no more than give him her last breath!

"In the evening, Conall dresses a funeral stone for them both, and sings the ritual lament. But the voice of Babd, the crow goddess, proclaims in the night that Cúchulainn is from now on in the Isle of Heroes, and is one of those who cannot die.

"Now all this happened the day of the feast of Samhain, at the beginning of the cold season of storms and rains, when the gods live with us, and the living communicate with the dead!"

The Seneschal, having risen, turned towards the sea, and said loudly: "As long as there are men who only become harp scrapers and have the heart of a rabbit! May the end of the hero Cúchulainn be an example to all who would live and die like him!"

Two days later in the twilight the *Cornwall* arrived in view of the coast of the great island of Britain. The last part of the voyage had been more eventful for they had to cross the terrible Blanchard current to the northeast of the Cotentin peninsula. Whatever the weather, whatever the state of the sky, the seas in this part of the world are full of currents and counter-currents. For miles and miles along an archipelago of breaking crests and eternal foam the waves swirl in mad disorder like water boiling in a pot. Merlin himself, who took the heavy rudder oar to direct the ship through this 'frying pan', and his mastery at the helm brought great admiration from the crew – with the exception of the Seneschal and his clan, who with obstinate bad faith refused to see any superiority in the bard.

On the way, the *Cornwall* joined the three vessels with the horses of the chiefs and the bulk of the expeditionary force, including the shock troops designated to give battle to Mordred.

King Arthur gave the order to the crew to haul down the sails and wait for night. The men descended to the banks of oars and a few archers were sent to land to kill any Saxon sentries charged with surveillance of the coast, to prevent them lighting fires on the hills of the Isle of Venta to give the alarm to the troops of King Kenric. The plan of the Breton chief was to sail round the isle under cover of darkness and disembark at Hanton, on the mainland, before dawn. He thought he would be able to reach Mordred's camp at Salisbury in less than five hours.

Merlin and Adragante, crouched in the front of the ship, whispered in the growing shadows.

"Dahut the Malefic of Ys is not dead," said the magus. "She is there haunting our shores and awaits each one of us. She is sometimes even within us. She is the sum of our ancient heredity, and that unknown seed that, from creature to creature, has descended as far as ourselves. It is for us to isolate the poison in that liquor that gives us life. And to merit regaining the heights for which we sometimes feel nostalgia, but to which we have lost the way in the night of our descent."

"Master," asked Adragante, "can I put a question to you?"

"Later," replied Merlin. "We will be fighting within four or five days. And until then I would like the chance to talk to you as man to man, which is also necessary."

There was a long silence. The wind freshened. The light of the heavens shone brightly in the firmament and the Milky Way seemed like a swarm of phosphorescent bees.

Merlin gazed long at the constellations and spoke as if in a dream: "Many of those worlds are extinct whose light we can see. The survival across space of a thing that lived and breathed like us – and from which we receive a posthumous message – is a proof of our communication with the dead. Nothing is lost in this immense universe All is written in the starlight.

"Our fleshly eyes are infirm, Adragante, but the day will come when we will see by the invisible light. And really know what constitutes for us mortals the beyond of today. Thus the walls of our cosmic prison will be removed but without benefit for the flight of our soul. The eyes of the soul alone have endless clarity, and men with bodies of clay will then be able to discover what we, the poets, have divined from 'the people of the seeds' who still sleep in the silos of Creation. For whoever conceives the arrangement of the universe, its first cause and its last end, the practical realisation is simply the labour of a workman by careful demonstration.

"A child would have been able to hold in the palm of his hand the seed of the oak tree from which this great mast was fashioned. But the initiate would already know that it would be the carrier of future sails to conduct the flower of Breton chivalry towards a certain strait…"

Merlin stopped. He felt the heart of his disciple beat more quickly and a shadow pass within his eyes.

The bard put his hand on that of Adragante. "Calm yourself, my son. I was going, in part, to answer the question you wanted to put to me. Have faith in me. Simply remember that birth is a death and death is a birth. When you came into this world you came in pain. The dedication of little importance. It is in you, in the palm of your hand, like the seed of the tree. But whatever happens, that event can do nothing to your spirit. It is for you to know how to wait the moment of God, if you are as worthy as I think you are."

"Then tell me quickly," murmured Adragante in an agitated voice.

"Do not be a child," replied Merlin. "You know very well I have never doubted your courage but the sacrifice of the true hero is not to escape in advance. It is a holy patience before the unknown. That hour will come, Adragante."

Driant de la Forest and Maret de la Roche were approaching.

"And what about them?" the impulsive Adragante could not stop himself from saying.

Merlin paused a moment, then at the thought that his reply could reassure his disciple he said: "It will come more quickly for them than for you."

The two young men, without knowing that he referred to them, greeted Merlin silently.

In the midst of the bustle on the *Cornwall*, here they were, the four of them, like travellers at a crossroads. Seeking in the shadows the fugitive face of friendship. Uniting their souls in the same flame without reproach. Merlin took the hands of the three knights and joined them one on the other. Then removed his golden torque, and on this living conjunction that symbolised the highest in human communication, he placed the five pointed star.

Warned of the landing of his father at Hanton, Mordred sent a courier to the Saxon King Kenric, and decided to wait for Arthur and his Bretons under the ramparts at Salisbury. Temporising allowed him to count on the arrival of his ally and his knights to decide the end of the battle.

The felon did not doubt that the victory would be hotly disputed. He also knew that he defended, along with the body of Queen Guenièvre, all the worldly goods for the possession of which he would not hesitate to be a parricide, as opposed to his adversaries, who were fighting for honour and would probably be massacred down to the last man before they abandoned their old King. Then there was Merlin who had known him since childhood and whose power he feared. Had not the mage already read his thoughts? Had he not warned Arthur of his alliance with Kenric and the Saxons?

But the instincts of the hunter succeeded in dismissing all this. He also had the short view of the barbarian, and raging ambition predominated over any other sentiment. Also in the uncertainty of what might come directly from 'the druidess's bastard', he resolved to concentrate on him from the start of the battle, driving his first attacks at Driant de la Forest, Maret de la Roche and Adragante, whom he knew were the favoured disciples of the bard.

In the meantime, with the New Moon of the last days of June, Arthur and his knights had come within a few miles of Salisbury. They elected to spend their evening together at a friendly manor, the attack on Mordred having been planned for the next morning at dawn.

In the main hall, built of granite, a great round table had been set for the last banquet of the Companions of the Round Table. Wax torches burned at the four corners of the hall, and the servants scurried to and from the kitchens, where in enormous chimneys there roasted whole sheep and legs of venison, in which hot peppers had been macerated with sea water.

In the gardens of the castle Merlin and Adragante were seated on the coping of a fountain waiting the call to dinner. The sun rested as if fixed at the zenith. The silence was only troubled by the intermittent call of a cuckoo, or the percussion of a woodpecker's beak on the oaks in the forest.

"Adragante my son," said Merlin, "you are going to sit for the third time at a feast of the Round Table. Until now, in our meetings, I have only spoken to your companions under the veil of symbol, but as it is possible that this banquet will be a farewell, it is to you, Adragante, the latest comer among the knights, that I must reveal certain things."

"A farewell banquet? Do you believe then, Master, that the invincible king of Brittany can be vanquished by Mordred?"

"Destiny," replied Merlin, "can take strange turns, and I have serious reasons to fear the worst, for all faults on this planet are repaid a hundredfold. Also, my duty from now on is to be silent on this point and to suffer the collective fate."

Adragante paled in looking at the Magus. Merlin placed his index finger, on which a ruby shone, before his mouth. Far off, southern breezes stirred the leaves of the wood whose confused mass barred the horizon.

"Listen," said the bard in a lower voice, "it is about Merlin that I am going to speak to you."

"About... you?" babbled the youth.

"Yes, about me. I am old, Adragante. The Sublime Father who had me born a long time ago has preserved the aging of men from me because I was destined to be at the confluence, on this Western land, of certain events that will change the course of history."

After a silence broken only by the clear song of a skylark lost in the blue of the evening, Merlin continued:

"Among all the blind who people this universe, I have been a visionary, a witness. For long years I was inducted in the religion of the ancestors. Initiated by the Druids, they raised me in the cult of Esus, god of eternal forces, personified by nature, by light and by heroism. In this theogony the law of Love was absent, and the esoteric significance of Woman, that great enigma of creation, did not appear in our rites. The priestesses represented not so much moral powers but rather forces of nature. Now, in awakening to the exterior world this marvellous flowing of symbols that constitute a great book of Nature, I have presented other truths than those taught me in the temples. Everywhere I saw only the law of the forest, and the strong triumphing perpetually over the weak, as in the wild exploits of Lugaid and Cúchulainn. There lacked a superior movement in the act of the hero, to legitimise or exalt his sacrifice. As for the woman, what was she beyond the functions of means whereby, or a reproducer?

"The more I thought, the more I was persuaded that only love – but a love absolutely different from that sung by our fathers – could enlighten and balance so many confused forces. But it was necessary that this Love be *incarnated* in a human being, and presented to the world as a teaching. Well Adragante, this man has existed. He died in the East four or five hundred years ago, and he passed his life, which was quite short, among courtesans, slaves and children of the people.

He entered and struggled against the powers of society, insulted the rich, the priests and the wielders of swords. He left an oral tradition, which would be consigned to scribes and of which all prescriptions can be resumed in three words: Renunciation, Sacrifice, Love.

"In the forests of Caledonia I met a strange traveller, whose name I will not say. He told me the life and the martyrdom of this extraordinary man, done to death for having preached forgiveness, who spent his last breath forgiving his executioners! This traveller affirmed that the man in question would be a god, or rather a son of god. But of what god? Would it be of Dianaff, the unknown god? But then how could a god accept to die like that? Or then, could it be that he is not god?"

Merlin was silent for a few seconds.

"It is true," he continued, "that other gods or sons of gods in history have known a death as cruel. Such as Pythagoras, the sage…"

"The one who was in touch with the Druids?"

"Yes. Our colleges had much in common with him. Ah well! If one believes Diogenes of Laërce, that supernatural man was burnt, in his house in Cretona with thirty eight of his disciples, who represented the spiritual chivalry of the times."

"That's terrible…"

"It's normal. For the Brute has an instinctive horror of anything he does not understand. And this new sage of the East must have learned this to his cost. The one who was crucified, it seems, by the same people whom he had healed on the roads of his country. His Greek name meant a cross or a fish. His favourite disciple would have received from him and written his secret doctrine in a surprising book. But that is not all. And now, Adragante, I need your closest attention…"

Merlin took Adragante's right hand in his own, and making sure that they were quite alone, continued with lowered voice:

"I saw that holy traveller several times. He had chosen to live in a hut of reeds in the Caledonian forest, and claimed to receive his food from the birds in the sky. At our last meeting, which was several seasons ago, he took me before a crude effigy he had hung in his cabin. It represented this son of god, completely naked and tied to a cross. And this is what he confided to me, saying that I appeared to be one of the few men worthy to hear and able to keep this secret.

"It was about a cup… a cup cut from a fabulous emerald. And in this cup, a certain Joseph of Arimathea collected the blood of this just man, that the lance of a soldier had caused to flow from his side when he was still on the gibbet. Now the traveller of Caledonia swore to me that this cup – or more exactly the vase containing this blood –

had been brought to Cornwall. That is to say the country where we now are. There is a miraculous virtue in this relic, but its possession is reserved for a pure heart. And it was to find this pure heart, worthy to touch this blood that had been spilt for the redemption of all men, that I founded the order to which you belong, and that I have called the Order of the Knights of the Round Table."

"But this sacred vase," asked Adragante the Gaël, "where is it?"

The magus put a finger to his lips again.

"It is in the West, the traveller confided to me. It has a name – a most mysterious name that I cannot reveal – but through it, future man will be released from mortal baseness, and woman, finally torn from her carnal servitude, will be encompassed with all the attraction of ideal love. For it is not only a matter of material possession of this sacred object. There will be an eternal seed, fallen from the lips of the Sage, of which only the letter has been passed on, but not the redeeming intention. And this is the last secret. Hear it…"

And the mage leaned towards the ear of his disciple, and there was only the still water and the bellbine growing in the fountain to hear his words…

Soon after, all were met about the symbolic Round Table. Merlin had King Arthur on his right and at his left Adragante the Gaël. Forty-seven knights were present. One seat remained empty, according to a tradition established by the mage. It was the custom to maintain silence until the end of the meal.

During the banquet, which was brief, Merlin looked in turn at all his companions, who by their valour or their virtues had been judged worthy to take part in this confraternity. There were elegant youths like Lucain, Maret de la Roche or Adragante; colossi like Guinebaud or Gauvain; wolves like Bliais du Chastel in whom Merlin had tamed the savagery; poets like Guivret de Lamballe, who fought only for the sole regard of a sky princess; and greybeard knights like Miladus or Bohor de Carhaix. Opposite Merlin sat Driant de la Forest, the most handsome of all perhaps with his leather coat studded with metal nails, his very black hair, his shining eyes that seemed to absorb all the light, and lips the colour of wild poppies.

During the meal the servers had only served water and a little barley beer to the diners. At a sign from the bard they brought wine that had been harvested from the hills of the Loire by Arthur's soldiers supervised by Merlin himself. The servers then retired and closed the doors.

Merlin rose and took from a casket a golden engraved cup that was set with nine rubies and a great emerald. He filled it with wine and raised it carefully to the level of his eyes.

"My friends, my children," he said, "this cup which we are going to bring to our lips contains the blood of both earth and sky. The star of the day and the star of the night have alternately caressed with their beams the grape from which it was pressed.

"We too are children of the same vine, and this cup represents our physical and spiritual harvesting. It is an emblem of sacrifice that the unknown Master from out of the sun has wanted to perpetuate, so that from now on the Temple may be purified from all human immolation. For you are no more willing victims, but foundation stones of the divine will. You have passed the bodily state that ends in the grave. You have been reborn to a second life.

"That is why, on the eve of this battle which forms part of the circle of Abred, that we men of flesh and blood delivered for the triumph of the spirit, do not say farewell, for we are together forever.

"Each one of us is nothing. The personality is but an illusion. It is only the work that counts, and that torch will pass from hand to hand until the end of the world. We are the spokes of a wheel whose centre is the light. The closer we are to the centre, the quicker we turn. The further away we are, the more we risk leaving the wheel. You who have received the seed will find supreme consolation. Death is an unimaginable dawn. The soul that has found God is forever delivered from the aspects of bodily life. It has passed to a higher kingdom."

The mage tendered the cup to the king who represented the Order of the Round Table.

"This cup is the symbol of divine sacrifice and the transmutation of the spirit into reborn souls. I drink to you, my king and my friend. I drink to you, my knights and my children. I drink to your death, to your deliverance, to your flight to eternal Love!"

They passed the cup from mouth to mouth. And Merlin refilled it nine times.

The knights having risen, the magus gave Adragante the symbolic kiss, which made the circuit round the companions of the Round Table.

Then at a call from Merlin the servers returned and extinguished the torches. The knights dispersed for a night's rest, their last perhaps before the great sleep.

IV

An hour later, Merlin had saddled his horse and was riding full tilt towards the Temple of the Druids. A great wind had risen and raised in the trees of the ancient forest an immense enclosed murmuring.

From time to time, when the moonlight pierced through the branches, the table of a dolmen or columns of rough stones could be seen pointing to the sky. Finally, under the shadowy vault, Merlin came to the sanctuary, surrounded by a belt of venerable oak trees. Here lived the Patriarch who ruled over all the colleges of Broceliande.

The bard with the golden torque had come to take leave of the priestly master he had not seen since the foundation of the Order of the Round Table. Another reason that brought him to the high priest was the fear that he might have offended the gods of his birth by favouring the appearance of a new religion on the earth of the ancestors.

The spell of this forest that had seen his birth enchanted him anew. He saw Koridwen, the white faery, gathering sellaginella and vervain. And Gwyon, the first poet, the Prometheus of the Celtic religion, whose father lived in Cassiopeia. Or suddenly appearing before him in a halo of lights, Esus the Terrible, Lord of the forest.

The memory of his mysterious birth came back to him, and he felt the blood of the druidess beating within him. Was he a renegade? Would the anger of the god of the forests strike him? Would he be expelled from the circle of happiness? Driven for ever from Gwynfyd? Had he been mistaken in the end?

A sweat of anguish flowed from him. In the full light of the moon, he saw his shadow on horseback, stretched across the grass. He pulled on the reins, dismounted, and advanced slowly toward the two ovates who, day and night, spear in hand, guarded the temple precincts.

As the ovates went to summon the Patriarch, Merlin crossed the threshold of the sacred place. As soon as he entered he suddenly rediscovered the atmosphere that had bathed him during his childhood and the long years of his novitiate. Nothing had changed since then. The circle was formed by quarters of rock and trunks of trees. A prodigious covering of bushes, of tamarisk and sea grass isolated the place from the outer world. At the end, thousand year old paths opened onto a natural grotto where the pontiff's smith guarded the perpetual fire that was extinguished each year on the night of the 1st and 2nd of November. A holy night, symbolising the periodic rebirth of the world, during which the god Samhan, judge of the deceased, came to sit in tribunal to decide the fate of the year's dead. A similar ceremony took place on the Holy island, not far from the Bay of Trépassés, where the nine Sènes priestesses officiated.

In evoking the sacred fire that the druidesses revived, the bard recalled the struggle he had undertaken against the feminine colleges that, little by little, had been corrupted by the practice of human sacrifice. In fact these daughters of the fire, originally beneficent, had become veritable furies who ceaselessly sought new victims, and reigned, knife in hand, halfway between lust and terror. A strange wild emulation, the obsession perhaps of some who wanted to lay themselves naked under the knife of these virgins, favoured this scramble toward the immolation stone.

And Merlin recalled, shuddering, the hymn these fanatics proclaimed before having their throat cut by the druidesses:

> My tongue will chant my song of death in the circle of
> stones that enclose the world.
> It is a feast between two lakes; a lake surrounds me, and
> about the circle, another girding circle of deep moats.
> A beautiful grotto is before me; the great stones conceal it.
> The serpent advances outside crawling toward the bowls
> of the druidess, of the druidess with the golden horns.
> The golden horn in her hand, her hand on the knife, the
> knife on my heart.

Merlin knew these serpents and their allies. He had tamed these two monsters. But despite their apparent submission, the priestesses, seeing the power of fascination that they had on the crowds diminish, cursed the bard and vowed him to the infernal gods.

Morgan, the sister of King Arthur, high priestess of the Isle of Sein, was one of the most relentless against the mage. Once she had dreamed of Merlin as a lover but, outraged by his indifference, now thought only of how to satisfy her passion by immolating him with her own hand.

The bard thought again of this network of malediction that never ceased to threaten him, when the Patriarch appeared before him.

He came out of a cabin made from silver birch covered with thatch; his realm and his universe, for the Druid doctrine required his permanent contact with the natural world. This individual was ageless, of spectral appearance, consumed by ages of austerity. Discarnate one could say, for he had no more humanity in his mummified face other than the living flame of his eyes and the two blue veins that ran, like a last light of life, under the priestly tiara of golden horns. In his bony hand, which came from his long white robe embroidered with purple silk, shone a sacred stone of great rarity with emerald reflections, which was used to help the transmigration of souls. Like Merlin he wore at his throat the star of initiation.

Seeing the bard, the high priest made a vague gesture of surprise and a kind of smile crossed his face.

"I was told of your presence," he said in a clear voice that contrasted with his otherworldly aspect, "and was awaiting you. What do you want from me, from us?"

He extended his hand in the direction of the grotto where the sacred fire burned.

Merlin did not reply. The impassiveness, the invitation from he who had inculcated him with wisdom, troubled him. Why this visit after so many years? Then he pulled himself together. He had come to seek more than advice, more than help, a revelation perhaps!

He looked long and deeply at the Patriarch.

After a long silence the latter said "Would you like to see the places of your childhood once more?"

And without awaiting a response from the bard he went under a vault of foliage, where Merlin followed him without a word. They soon came to a large hut, brightly lit, before which a druid watched.

"Enter," said the Patriarch, "under the roof of the Red Branch. You will not see idols as in your new religion, for the image of god that we carry within us is untranslatable, but perhaps your search for the past will awake before the banners and trophies to the glory of the god of armies that watch here. Look at the gold ingots in which universal cupidity is condensed and whose circulation we forbid. Are you sure that the priests whose message your curiosity has sought will prevent the future world from cutting its throat for their possession? By what right do you answer for the future?"

"Master," replied Merlin, "I cannot answer for the future any more than you can for the present. The God-Force cannot divide its power between two brothers who are at each other's throats. And trophies are sometimes only the spoils of oppressed justice."

"The Force is of divine origin, Merlin. Look at the example of the sacred trees. Too bad for those which cannot reach the heights! They die stifled and will be reborn elsewhere."

"But there are the Caesars who fell your oak trees and who sell your virgins at auction. Is their force divine?"

44

"They can do nothing against us. Our theocracy has defied their tyranny."

"You admit then, Master, that there is a force superior to the Force?"

"No doubt, and all my life is witness to that truth."

"Then what do you call that Force which makes the victim able to dominate his executioner?"

"The Light-Force of Wisdom. Do you have another name for it?"

"Yes. Love."

A great astonishment passed through the eyes of the Pontiff.

"Allow me to be surprised," he continued in a more serious voice, "that you have been able to forget natural law at this imperative point. To love your executioner is an aberration. You have understood it so well that you were the first to stand against human sacrifice, and that has brought you mortal enemies. Do you know that?"

Merlin bowed his head.

"And here you are," pursued the old druid, "you, the initiate whom I thought my equal, and worthy one day to cut the mistletoe with the golden sickle, and you take an infamous gibbet as a sign of 'redemption', and go on to permit, for the glorification of a victim, the monstrous exploitation of a part of the human race for the sake of the future. You sow resignation and servitude. You prepare the hecatombs of your friends."

"Has the religion of my ancestors, to which I remain faithfully attached," replied Merlin, "prevented Mordred from drawing the sword against his father? Forbidden the massacre being prepared at Salisbury?"

At this point it seemed to Merlin as if the shadow of the Patriarch grew immeasurably under the roof of the Red Branch. The fire of his gaze became phosphorescent. He put his parchment like hand to the star of his golden torque and slowly pronounced, "This battle that you think lost all depends on you, Merlin, to lose it. You will not be able to sing the bardic chant as at other times. You do not believe in your heart of hearts the omnipresence of the God-Force. You have crumpled your solar power. You are haunted by the spectre of a crucified…"

"Whose passion," interrupted Merlin, "whose sublime lesson you refuse to hear, and who is only the last and most striking in a line of heavenly messengers. Other initiates, whose names irradiate our souls, have prefigured by a bloody death the symbol of the lamb. All were victims, but triumphant victims, who live forever on the dust of the executioners."

"Believe me, my son," continued the Pontiff without responding to Merlin, "you have compromised the victory of your brothers, because the germ of resignation has entered your heart. You will not sing the bardic chant as before, Merlin. The golden apples are fallen. The silver harp is no more than a harp of grief. Your companions of the Round Table will perish, Merlin, because you have loved them too much. Love is the brother of Death. Remember, my son, the stone of equilibrium and its point of liberty. Love kills Liberty."

"Death is nothing," said Merlin. "You have taught me that yourself at other times, that death is the milieu of a long life. I see again in the Hieroglyphs that fill this circle devices that teach the scorn for death."

"Then why, in these conditions, come to seek help for your disciples? What does the death of Adragante matter? Have you not chanted with him: *'If we die like Bretons, we never die too soon!'*"

Merlin said nothing. The Patriarch had clearly touched him. Without adding a word, the latter took a naphtha lamp and opened a side door, gesturing for the bard to follow him. They came to another hut, more in shadow this time.

"Do you recognise it?" asked the Pontiff, protecting the flame with his emaciated fingers.

"Yes, the house of sadness and anguish."

They entered. The passing of the lamp lit up plaques of metal, each engraved with a swastika, symbol of the solar wheel and the luminous accomplishment of being. In the shadows could be discerned couches garnished with dead leaves, and on little tables, small bottles, horns and strange instruments.

"I would prefer," said Merlin quietly, "to see my disciples survive and for me die in their place. They are my initiates, the key-carriers of the future."

"The initiates of your new message, Merlin? The testament of the Essenian?"

"No," responded the bard sharply. "The two testaments united. Yours and His!"

"I never make innovations," said the old man. "The oral tradition of our temples suffices me. And the image of the sacred tree. What will become of the mistletoe if it is separated from the oak? Are you not already the prey to the vertigo of dogma, the sterile dialectics of Kimri Pélage, on the doctrine of predestination? And in other times, my son, you would have had no need of us to render Adragante invulnerable or to dispute his death. You know as well as our brothers the occult forces of nature, the virtue of plants and venoms, levitation, ceremonial magic, and the secret of those stones that the vulgar call 'precious'."

He indicated his gem.

"It is like that to be attached to humans," continued the patriarch. "By virtue of the lesson of love, the Enchanter has doubted, and has lost the secret of his enchantments. He will thus accept our mediation in this circumstance, that his disciple Adragante, in the event of a mortal wound, will be saved by our healing magi?"

Merlin, without response, firmly shut his eyes. A light shone in the gaze of the Pontiff.

"So be it," he said. "If the battle is fatal to your friend…"

"To two of my friends," corrected the Enchanter. "To King Arthur and to my disciple Adragante the Gaël."

"If the battle is fatal to your two friends, sound this horn that I give you, and at night I will send the Temple servers. On one condition however…"

The two men faced each other for some seconds. Merlin folded his arms and awaited the shock.

"If you call me," said the Patriarch, "it would be on the understanding that you return to the religion of your ancestors."

⁛

Merlin had reached the way out in silence when the Pontiff laid a hand on his shoulder.

"I cannot let you go," he said slowly, "without making a revelation… an important one. Will you, before going to rejoin your companions spend a few moments with me?"

The patriarch closed the door on the bard, showed him to a stool and invited him to sit.

"Faithful to the rules of the priesthood, you have never, beyond the teaching I have given you, asked me any questions about yourself or the mystery of your birth.

"No doubt in the course of your life, where you have merited wearing the blue sash and become the greatest initiate and the most inspired in the Island of Britain, you have sometimes felt at the bottom of your deepest memory a division, which despite your spiritual ascension, ceaselessly called you back to the curiosities of the natural world.

"You belong, my son, to the race of seers. You are *awendhyon*, that is to say endowed with the second sight, and that is the Spirit that breathes in your soul. Often you have recalled the past, and have been called to read in the book of the future. But in your destiny there hovers an immense shadow that is interposed between you and your solar spirit. Strange desires, that crowd in on you violently, subsist in your interior self, and you sometimes regret, when sleeping, not being able to have your fill of the things of the earth. It floats on and around you, this nostalgia of a regret.

"It prevents you from having attained the last circle of initiation. You have not yet passed the great night of renunciation. You are a poet, Merlin, I would say a man of sorrows. You know only the intermittence or the recurrence of enlightenment. You do not contemplate the absolute light in a final serenity.

"Have you not come, to take an earthly incident, to put a dilemma before yourself that obliges you to put everything to question? And that troubles the mirror of your soul.

"In the name of the Holy Triad of which I am here the servant, I therefore ask you to hear me. And for this interview, that I know will be our last, to gather all the spiritual force of your being. Do not interrupt me. Be as calm as if you had already crossed the abyss of death."

Impassively, Merlin signed to the Pontiff that he was ready.

"Whatever," continued the Patriarch, "the result of this imminent battle, assuming that the gods wish to play out our prevision, and whatever decision you take on leaving here for the conduct of your life, it is the last time, Merlin, that you will take part in the bloody events of a conflict. Your mission as a bard is over.

"It remains for you to test yourself in the solitude of the forests, rediscovering the pact with nature, but this time knowing the secret of your origins. With an eye that knows how to look at nature, a heart that knows how to feel nature, a spirit that dares to follow nature, you will make the way of an adept through the mineral, vegetable, animal and starry worlds. And as woman is the supreme animal, and at the same time the reflection in the flesh of the unknown Goddess, she will be the supreme portal for your initiation. In knowing a woman, you will discover the depths of nature. And if the initiate is capable of the mastery, will overcome your desire for ever. Perhaps too you will rediscover Morgane. But at this moment nothing can penetrate your diamond-hard armour."

The Patriarch rose, and taking from a casket a silver ring encrusted with rubies, he offered it to Merlin.

"Here, my son, is the ring that belonged to your mother, whom you have never known. She died a long time ago, amongst we who, all her life, protected her from the reprobation that surrounded her for giving birth to a son when she had been a vestal in one of our temples, without ever having been with any man. Here, Merlin, is a dark secret that you can perhaps discover for yourself in the future. Angel or demon, you will doubtless know. But, for me, who knew your mother well, it seems certain that you were not engendered with the seed of a man. Truth finally obliges me to reveal to you that at the moment of your birth, a fanatical monk, who had betrayed our good faith – and who wanted to protect you from a malefic heredity – poured on your forehead the water of baptism."

At these last words of the Pontiff Merlin had closed his eyes.

The old man, without another word, opened the door on the moonlight and blew out his lamp.

A few moments later, Merlin, the horn in a bandolier and holding in his hand the maternal ring, remounted his horse and left at a gallop for the castle where the Knights of the Round Table were still quartered for the night.

V

As he rode through the night, passing from the milky clarity of crossroads to the shadow of forest ways where tracks known only to himself deadened the sound of his passing, Merlin felt his heart gripped with a still unproven bitterness. The secret of his birth, that he had always suspected, was from now on confirmed for him.

What is more, his mission as bard was coming to an end. The Patriarch had been definite, the hour of testing sounded like the lunar dial that shone above like a woman's face, half hidden behind the high drapery of the sky.

Before him, beyond the scented breath that rose from that summer night he also sensed the odour of a nearby mass grave, and as he slowed his mount he heard a convulsive cry, a cry of an animal with cut throat, that shattered the silence of the woods. His horse reared and refused to go on.

Before him at the edge of a clearing was an eagle owl as big as a man, deploying with a dull sound its wings striped with moonbeams, suspended in space at the height of his horse's head whose four hooves remained fixed to the ground.

Under the horns that surmounted the enormous round head, the bard saw two phosphorescent eyes that stared at him fixedly. Then the night eagle advanced its black hooked beak toward Merlin, and gave a long sigh, almost in his face, and said in a deep voice: "Man is foolish ... man is mad ... Stay with us ... Houihou ... hou-hou!" and rose straight up like a flame to the starry sky with a howl of laughter.

Merlin had not yet recovered from his stupor when he heard chanting, in a raucous woman's voice, that came into the starry night from the shadows of a copse. He remembered then that not far from this clearing, called that of the Unicorn, there was a convent of druidesses. Still quite overcome by the encounter with the eagle owl, the horseman dismounted and walked towards the voice, which became less and less delirious, swelling now in vociferous fury.

At the end of a narrow path, in a wide circular space that opened between the trees, like a perfect sphere in the moonlight, an oblong stone table was mounted on four vertical stones, lit by the flames of three torches. One of these torches was fixed to the trunk of a gigantic oak, the other two held by two women, scantily dressed in black robes that opened at their thighs and also revealed their breasts. Both had their eyes closed, their hair falling to their shoulders. Their lips, shining like blood, as if daubed with berries of belladonna, opened on pink gums and cried out violently rhythmic syllables in response to the imprecations of their leader. As still as stone idols, they guarded the entrance to a long rectangular hut closed with a leather curtain. Two enormous wolfhounds lay before their bare feet. As he approached, Merlin saw that the clearing was surrounded by a large trench furnished with sharp spears, over which the footbridge had been withdrawn.

The third priestess, she who shrieked before the dolmen, had not seen Merlin arrive. She stood in profile, almost naked, her wheat coloured hair breaking over her breasts, in a short dark robe belted at the waist with a copper serpent. At her side hung a golden billhook. Crowned with vervain she kept her great blue-green eyes obsessively fixed on the entrance to the hut. Her high breasts, full and rising toward the distended veins of her neck, pointed their nipples toward the bloody light of the torches. In her right hand she held a long triangular knife. Near her, on a stool, shone a large bronze cauldron. Another human sacrifice was about to take place in this secret part of the forest.

The magnetic stanzas of the druidess called for the victim. Her voice, by turns tender and despotic, demanded blood to appease the spirits of the gods.

For the victim panting and naked
Death is sweet under the steel of a naked virgin
Come, my love, to my arms of snow.

The snow boils… Death is warm in my arms.
When the springs of the heart gush your coral blood
You will keep forever the honey of my kisses
And my look of fire will split you to the core.
Let us go then, son of the Earth, come naked under the stars.
Give your blood for our cruel love,
Give your love for the smile of Bel,
Come to my blade, child, offer your body
And my virgin breast will suckle you in death!

The priestess suddenly stopped, her call ending like a death rattle. Then from inside the hut a beating drum was heard, sounding like a tom-tom, and a voice rose from behind the leather curtain.

Suffering is nothing
If it is under the lightning of your eye.
To die is nothing
If it is through the naked arm of the virgin.
Penetrate me, tear me to the heart
That the god may gather me in his tent
As you receive me in your breast.
I am here!

One of the guardians of the threshold pulled back the curtain. A naked man appeared, his hands tied behind his back. He was young, almost beardless, and his face assumed a frenzied expression. Behind him came two druidesses who held over his head the double sexed god with a bull's face.

"Stop!" cried Merlin.

At his imperious voice, the priestesses gave a cry and extinguished their torches in the lustral water, while the sacrificer, with flaming eyes, tried to see into the night what could be the trouble.

"Go back, pig!" she cried. "Who are you who dares to trouble the mysteries of Koridwen?"

"These are not the mysteries of Koridwen," replied the bard. They are abominable orgies, where you try to inflict on a man the mastery that escapes you. You are amazons of the night, daughters of Hecate. You practice a degenerate cult that has nothing in common with the divine oracles of Voluspa…"

"Now I recognise you," cried the priestess. "You are Merlin, the bard with the golden torque, the lyre carrier of King Arthur! You have already entered a struggle with the Pontiff. You call yourself a bringer of I know not what message of love and pity. You want to put an end to the cult of the ancestors. To disown your maternal blood!"

"No one is more respectful than me for the male god and the Holy Triad that flames in the immaculate ether! You, on the other hand, daughter of the shadows, you and your companions have wanted to substitute the cult of the solar god with that of inferior gods who feed on your lust and cruelty! You have wanted to rule by terror. You have dreamed of emasculating the Sublime Father. And you have multiplied the sacrifices, replacing the blood of animals with that young man of your race!"

"You heard him! All our victims are consenting! They burn to die at our hands!"

"Because you have perverted the will of the faithful. It's enough! I intend to put an end to these hideous ceremonies. I am come to face you as one who fights for the light, like the son of the priestess of Apollo before the fury of the Bachantes. But I will overcome you. I will abolish your reign of murder and blood!"

"You will succumb like the son of the priestess of the South. We will tear you apart with our nails!"

Then suddenly she cried: "Sabag! ... Vanao! Release the dogs on the traitor! Tear him to pieces! We will see if the male god protects him!"

The two wolfhounds leaped from the shadows, tongues hanging out, their teeth shining in the moonlight. With a bound they cleared the trench, barking, and stretching their steaming mouths toward the bard's throat.

But he stepped back a pace, and without batting an eyelid, described with his two extended arms the arc of the protective circle of the adepts. And with all his will stiffened to break the malefic threat, he simply commanded briefly:

"Peace ... Sabag, Vanao! At my feet!"

Overcome, the two beasts lay before the magus, muzzles pressed to the ground.

At this, in the clearing, the druidess howled and ground her teeth. It was the first time her demonic power had been broken by a superior will.

Merlin turned to remount his horse.

She threw herself on the stone and cried to him while brandishing her knife:

"Go, Merlin, go! Defender of consecrated victims. Go to the carnage you have prepared for your brothers! Double hearted man! You are upset by our stone of sacrifice but will sing tomorrow on the battlefield to immolate your friends, your disciples, all for the murderous passion of a chief. Don't you realise that your delinquent sensitivity prepares centuries of slaughter for future humanity? Lyre carrier of misfortune! The sun about to dawn will set on your downfall. For having doubted the God of the strong. For having betrayed the holy truths of which we are guardians. You are going to watch the throat cutting of the Knights of the Round Table you have brought to our dolmens. Tomorrow night, the sun you adore will scorn you. You will be no more than a lost dog. You will fly alone like a cursed man or a leper!

"Go Merlin, go with your rabbit's heart and spill the precious blood of the man who was frightened. But take care for yourself! Beware of Sklera, the priestess! We will meet again. The forest is ours, do you hear? One day we will bind you to this same stone. Your flesh will know the kiss of the knife. You will die from our nocturnal caresses. And you will be our finest offering to the lunar divinities that you have rejected. And we will give your genitals for our dogs to eat!"

At that moment an arrow whistled past Merlin's head and struck in the bark of an oak beside him. He pulled it out, and turned back toward Sklera.

"Farewell!" he said. "I take your message!"

And pressing his mount with his knees he galloped off into the night.

Alone once more, whipped by the stimulating air of the coming morning that arose from the hills, Merlin reflected. Merlin was troubled, without the power to collect himself together. The sight of that naked man with his face tense with voluptuous pleasure, who had come to offer himself to the knife of a priestess, obsessed him. He who had never been tormented with thoughts of physical love, had felt the influence of this wild creature, beautiful as the night star, whose kisses brought death. Living belladonna of the forests, poisonous daughter with milk-like arms, whose embrace brought the vertigo of the abyss. What strange anxiety bit him to the heart? And from where did these unknown feelings come that arose in his body?

Suddenly, beyond the forest, a pink and gold band announced the coming of day. The stars dimmed. Merlin, his heart torn, heard the last imprecations of Sklera. She had spoken truly when she had predicted the massacre today, of which he was the lyrical instigator. What difference was there indeed between the raised knife of the druidess and this harp, whose strings would be sticky with blood? Was it for the Sublime Father, or to assuage the crude passion for combat, that would deliver the javelin or the spear to the youth of Adragante? What could he do?

The manor appeared at the bend in the valley. In the great paved courtyard, still cast in shadow, he could hear the snorting of horses and the rolling out of war chariots. Breastplates shone between the banners, and Merlin's ear caught the brief guttural commands, and the clash of arms.

When the bard dismounted Adragante stood before him in his coat of mail with his heavy sword at his side. He had the air of a legendary hero with the hair of an angel. And the bow he carried on his left shoulder, like a wing, accentuated his likeness to the archer of love. In his leather belt he had tucked arrows made from branches of wild elm, and he carried in its case the harp of the magus that would give the signal for battle.

Merlin shuddered on receiving the seven stringed lyre invented by Orpheus to sing the poetry of the world and tame wild beasts, but which in his own hands would become an instrument of death.

"Master," said Adragante, "here is the harp that will lead us to war and to victory. I will watch you for the moment of attack. Sing for us. Sing for the triumph of justice. Sing for King Arthur and for the glory of Celtica!"

"Aren't you afraid of dying?" asked the mage.

"No, not with you, not in front of you. When you are there I'm never scared. And anyway, why die? You who know everything, do you think that the time may have come for the last goodbye?"

"I don't know," said Merlin, turning his head away. "Try to keep near me during the fight."

"Impossible. I am chosen to guard the king."

"Then God go with you!" said the bard with a sigh.

He faltered before this innocent. Such assurance frightened him.

"Death is a birth," went on the young knight. "It was you, Master, who taught me that, the other night on the bridge of the *Cornwall*. I will never forget, either, your last toast to all the companions who will no longer come to sit at a feast of the Round Table."

"Well, so be it!" said Merlin. "If then you die in the fight I will meet you in the heavenly Lyre that shines in the northern sky. But if it is I who should go, remember the symbolic cup and the lesson of eternal love. Nothing lasting down here is made without the heavenly fire.

And only that which is made without it is destined to perish! Your having been initiated, my child, is as if I had given you the Pole Star to guide you through the dark. Go your way from now on without fear or reproach. But for now, farewell!"

Merlin gave the accolade to his disciple in exchanging a last look with him.

Far off, the Korn-boud sounded the assembly in the full light of day. The green hills of the Island of Britain stretched out like fleece in the calm freshness of the dawn, as King Arthur appeared, mounted on his black steed, holding his sword Escalibor up to the rising sun and holding against his breast a shield in the form of a boat, upon which leaped the dragon of St Efflam.

Prancing around him, the knights of the Round Table formed a forest of lances and standards. They wore leather skirts, sparkling steel breastplates and their shields made livid splashes of colour here and there. Some wore a helmet like a wolf's mouth surmounted by a mane, others favoured a boar's head edged with cock feathers. Bright emerald or sea green eyes shone from under red or blond hair flowing down to their shoulders. Some were clean shaven in the Roman manner; others, arms and knees bare, tanned by the sun and sea air, had bushy moustaches like muzzles of wild beasts. Great men by necessity, formed by storms and hard winters, polished like pebbles by the kisses of the sea, impulsive and impatient, humble and finicky, credulous and disbelieving, cruel and magnanimous, they were a race of Argonauts of the North, their gaze ever raised to the stars, embarked on a quest for the golden fleece, over the eternal waves of the sea.

Merlin, who rode at the head of the column, plucked the strings of his lyre. Trumpets broke the silence with their strident call. And the expeditionary force from Armorica, with its knights and archers, its spearmen and sling throwers, its wagons and chariots pulled by oxen and stags, its huntsmen and various footmen, soon disappeared, hidden by the forest, in a great cloud of sunlit dust.

VI

The two armies met on Salisbury Plain, a little way from Camblan, where Mordred had assembled his own.

According to custom, the troops massed behind their chief, staying some distance apart to weigh each other up before actual engagement. Knights could be heard drawing their swords, archers adjusting their arrows, and the clash of arms over the calm of the plain seemed like the tuning up of an orchestra before the start of a barbarous symphony.

A terrible moment came when Arthur and Mordred exchanged glances.

Face to face with him at two hundred yards, the Breton king looked on the astonishing villain he had brought into the world, mounted on a chestnut horse before an immobile swarm of rebel troops that covered the hill as far as the horizon. His sin of former times, the sin of his blind flesh, incarnated in this pale and bony dark knight. His enemy, his son and brother, who fondled with a parricidal hand the sword that hung from his steel clad thigh.

Arthur shivered. For the first time in his life perhaps, he felt the mysterious fear of a fate that exceeded his fortune. He the conqueror, a living legend, who had led 180,000 knights and 400,000 men at arms to victory after victory, suddenly felt the flaw in his destiny. He was no longer the Breton Siegfried piercing with blows of his lance the giant stavers-in of boats or flame-vomiting dragons. He now had to exterminate a monster he had himself spawned from the seed of his ancestors.

He bowed his head. Over there Mordred raised his sword toward the sky and the legionaries, trained in the school of Saxons, grouped into a triangle, presenting a compact mass bristling with lances and throwing spears. Suddenly this wall of bronze sounded forth a great cadenced clamour that sounded at moments like the cries of wild beasts. It was the war song of the Germans, that Tacitus has said "would frighten to death the birds of the sky", the baying of a multitude that made one think of an innumerable pack of wolves howling for meat.

Then Merlin, who had been looking at the king for several minutes and who had divined the fear in his soul, felt an old instinct re-awaken in his heart, of pride and of the fight. Before him rose the face of his country. There could be no quarter for ferocious beasts! And who knows? Perhaps one could strike a blow against the odds and change the stars of destiny. The Sublime Father could not abandon a just cause. They needed to win.

Merlin took his lyre, and in a powerful voice that dominated the surging of the enemy song, improvised his last bardic chant:

He who has raised his sword against his father
Will fall on his face to the ground in his blood.
The sea crow will eat his eyes
And the Scorpion lodge its sting in his heart.

The burden of shame is heavy to carry,
Heavy to carry, the pouch in the night of souls.
The soul of traitors is in the spume of the shadows
A dragnet full of rotten fish.

For me, my companions, our fearless knights
Fight here for the honour to live.
You are the harvest and bunches of grapes in the sky
And the Graal will meld with your crimson blood.

Strike, fierce spear, the horde of thieves,
Hanging hooks pierce their entrails.
One against ten we crush the barbarian dogs
And if we die, will die laughing.

At the banquet of death, the Table is round
Death is a faery, crowned with stars
May she receive us to her velvet breast
That we rule with her in the blue night.

The choir of six thousand warriors sang behind Merlin, to the clash of swords striking on shields, and the roaring of this western song of triumph. Merlin set himself on the neck of his horse, and raising his lyre with its sparkling strings, let fly the last arrow of his song and his steely gaze on the enemy chief.

A flash of second sight revealed to him the inevitable.

Did he not know that sorrow was a necessary contrast, the counterbalance to the element of triumph, and death the chrysalis of a soul called to the light? He understood that it had been necessary to compromise with evil, to sow in barbarian hearts the seed of honour, and project on a world prone to chaos the force and idea of chivalry.

Had he not learned in the temples that a metal in fusion, after it had boiled, suddenly congealed, far from the central fire, a prisoner of its own law, which is to harden on cooling. So a soul with a high destiny can compact in matter, by moving away from its divine Principle.

But the laws of equilibrium are ineluctable. The wall of the material, last frontier of nothingness, provokes a return shock. The very impulse to plunge into the shadows determines a return to the surface. Such is the way of things. The last stage of involution provokes the saving evolution.

Merlin saw Mordred the Cursed in the act of drawing his bow to give the signal to attack. He read now, as in a book, the springboard of this shadowed soul, devoted entirely to hate. And yet this monster was perhaps also necessary for the equilibration of certain hidden forces, bringing the Evil Angel to Redemption.

This must pay that. The world only advances at a price. What then brought the entail of a day of misfortune in the eternal cycle of things? Night succeeds day, as storm the blue sky, and felicity is a daughter of sorrows. An eclipse would never abolish the sun. And if the Bretons were massacred and driven from the Island of Britain, they would carry their transmigrated soul to the holy forests of Armorica. The soul of a people never dies, any more than life can be separated from its essence. Arthur, the Breton king, could never perish.

At that moment an arrow whined past the ear of the bard and struck the breastplate of Maret de la Roche.

It was the signal for battle. Arthur raised his sword. A sudden turbulence came over all. A couching of lances made the oriflammes flutter, and like a roll of thunder the Breton cavalry charged.

The spectre of Cain hovered over the battlefield, now burning under the rays of a torrid sun. Like all battles in history that put to grips brothers that come from the same womb, the hand to hand fighting grew quickly to an extraordinary ferocity.

The king, who before the engagement was closely supported by his best lieutenants, gave the order to the Seneschal and Driant de la Forest to advance the cavalry on the two wings of Mordred's army. As for himself, keeping Adragante at his side, and Maret de la Roche and most of the knights to make a rampart of living flesh, he wanted to charge at the centre. To attack Mordred and his chiefs of staff to disarticulate the rebel legions, breaking the fighting front with the first blow.

He counted on his faithful Cambrian archers, the best in the West, to throw back the Saxon spearmen, who fought half naked, proud to show their broad red or white chests, covered with scars. Dismegans and his five hundred archers lay on their backs to draw back their bows, applying their feet to the interior curve and pulling the string back to the chin with both hands. A cloud of sharp arrows struck the first rank of Saxons. Men with bloodied bodies pulled out the arrow heads with the cries of enraged beasts. Then the javelins responded.

The Breton knights who had broken against the bronze wall of the enemy came back at the charge. Mordred, scratched on the shoulder by an arrow of Dismegans, set his horse at a gallop on the group around his father. Swords shone in the light. The mêlée became diabolic. A crimson vapour from open wounds and the sweat of bodies, and breath from the steaming nostrils of confused horses, rose in the dust gilded by the sun.

Between midday and three o'clock this frightful tide came to the full. The companies of Mordred weakened, although superior in numbers. Arthur, wounded in the left arm by a barbarian, his blue belt stained with blood, crossed swords with Mordred without being able to strike him.

The Saxon infantry retreated towards the hill, before the impetuous vigour of the Bretons. Ardent breath merged as they spat threats and insults. The rebels sought the eyes of their enemies with their spear thrusts. Before dying, a javelin planted in his entrails, a Breton struck down three Saxons with blows of his axe.

Cut off heads rolled on the ground, eyes wide open, while their decapitated bodies stayed in the saddle, waving their arms. The hooves of rearing horses crushed this debris spurting teeth and brains. The drunkenness of this human grape harvest spread like a collective madness on the furious, like swarms of flame. A completely naked Saxon was pinned with his javelin to the shield of King Arthur. Maret de la Roche split his back with a terrible blow of his spear. They saw the body detach, the spinal column bursting open in a jet of blood, like the stern post of a back broken ship.

A young Breton, lying on a heap of bodies, had his breast opened with the blow of a lance. And in this hiatus of palpitating flesh his heart still beat, pumping out its last crimson streams. The guttural cries and screams of agony intermixed. The mercenaries called to each other in unknown languages. Babel rebuilt in an arena of coagulating blood and scattered limbs. The rebels fought, dagger between their teeth, handling with vertiginous ease the hooked spear whose crescent pierced the flesh and tore it in strips.

In about four hours, as the ranks of the two armies scattered, the fierceness of the fighting weakened, and the carnage took on a somnambulistic aspect. A terrible thirst tormented the dishevelled men, covered with wounds, harvesters of living flesh for so many hours! From one part to another, they felt the need for a truce, even though the issue of the battle remained undecided. For certain, the troops of Mordred had lost their bite. The Saxon line, broken on the left wing, had beaten a retreat towards the crest of the hill, where the felon's lieutenants sought to reform. The Breton infantry harassed them, but lacked sufficient reserves, the army of King Arthur could not renew its fund of heroism indefinitely.

Many knights of the Round Table had fallen. The white haired Miliadus, stomach opened with the blow of a lance, expired, his head on a flat stone, retaining his entrails with his two mailed fists. Bohor de Carhaix, face split in the middle, lost his lower jaw, which hung on his breastplate like a monstrous crop, and raised to the sky a face swollen and inflamed. Guinebaud, scalped by a sword, fell from his horse crying: "At the traitors! Victory to King Arthur!"

The Seneschal fought long against three Saxons who had cut the front legs of his horse. Once on the ground, he successfully pierced the throat of one of his adversaries, but having slipped in a pool of blood, he fell, and despite his Herculean strength, was mastered by the two rebels. One of them put his knee on this chest and the other gouged out his eyes with the butt of a spear. Driant de la Forest, charging too late to save the king's foster brother broke the heads of the two barbarians. The Seneschal rallied. Two streams of blood ran down the hollow of his cheeks.

Driant de la Forest leaned over him: "It's me, Driant … do you want a drink?" he asked him.

"Yes, then finish me off," responded the hunter of Broceliande. "End my life. I shall never fondle the breasts of Yveline again."

"Think of your soul, Seneschal, and of Gwyfyd" Merlin said to him, leaping from his horse to find in a helmet a little stagnant water.

"My soul," cried the Seneschal in a last rally, "I leave to the vultures, when they have sucked out the bone marrow of my enemies. Farewell!"

And taking the dagger that hung at his side, he cut open his coat, and groping around for a second plunged the blade into his heart up to the hilt.

Merlin, regaining his saddle, came towards Arthur and the last group of knights. He looked for his disciple Adragante, whom he had seen gallop a little while before, hair streaming in the wind, lying over his saddle tree.

However the king was resolved to strike the decisive blow. Mordred was the damned soul of this merciless combat. Invulnerable and volatile demon, he slipped between the swords, and arrows seemed to blunt themselves against his supple breastplate. He came surging out of the most murderous mêlées, and his hyena like cries ceaselessly restored the courage of his bodyguard.

It was necessary to defeat Mordred at any price. At a sign from Merlin Arthur regathered his companions.

"Mordred's hour has come!" he cried in the middle of the din. "Follow me, my friends! Have no other thought, just one objective, the death of the traitor. He should only die by my hand. But I give you leave to do so, who have clean hands. With him fallen, we will have the victory. Forward, and to the glory of God!"

For Merlin, the fight between Arthur and Mordred unfurled exactly like a dream of dreadful monotony, in which he had lived through all the episodes one by one. All was accomplished, like an already written drama, in which the actors ran to a foreseen denouement.

Miliadus bathing in his blood, the savage death of the Seneschal, the fearful collision of those maniacs who leaped among the sparks of the swords, Merlin saw all the fatalities inscribed in that immutable decor of blue sky, purple heather and gorse scorched in the sun. He knew that nothing could stop the game of Necessity, that the light of the spell had stripped it bare. The thunder was here, he heard its rumblings beyond the hill like the footfalls of the legions of fate.

Before this absurd wall, as high as the sky, all his magnetic force was annihilated. He looked sadly at his lyre across the withers of his horse, and searched again for the face of Adragante in the bloodied mud that remained of this confused mêlée. Then having touched, like a talisman, the horn that the Pontiff had given him, he followed Arthur and his knights who were about to sweep down on Mordred.

Would this last attack of the Breton chief decide the victory? Before the fury of the knights, Mordred retreated, while his lieutenants fell under their assailants' steel. His horse, wounded in the chest, threatened to unseat him. A long rumble of panic grew in the ranks of the Saxon army. Some barbarians opened their veins with their knives, others threw down their arms.

"Death to the traitor! Victory!" cried Driant de la Forest, almost with his knees on the neck of his horse. But at that moment a group of knights charged from the summit of the crest, soon followed by another swarm, haloed in dust, their lances profiled against the sky. Merlin gave a long groan. He recognised the advance guard of King Kenric's army coming to the aid of Mordred. There was a minute of stupor in the ranks of the Bretons. The resounding roar of battle remained poised like the prolongation of an organ note. And Mordred, profiting from the surprise, regained his saddle and galloped full tilt toward the reinforcements.

Arthur and his companions realised they were going to die. They beat a retreat and backed against a line of rocks that closed off the west side of a circle of greenery, and awaited the shock of the enemy.

Then the butchery restarted. The fresh troops of Kenric broke in successive waves on the Bretons exhausted by hours of combat. An unequal struggle in which the peninsular heroes, planted like breakwaters, performed prodigies and succumbed one after the other without attempting for a single moment to escape their cruel fate. They were the iron of the anvil, and forged, even in defeat, the indomitable race, the future race of steel.

The massacre lasted until sunset. Dismegans, chief of the archers, fought more than an hour, standing before a pile of bodies. Finally the axe of a mercenary split him in two to the belt. Kantalor, the sling shotter, cut the throats of eighteen enemies after disembowelling their horses. A kick in the head laid him out in a hedge of bindweed spangled with his blood.

The flower of knighthood fell about the king. After Bliais du Chastel, stunned like an ox by a mass of arms, it was Guivret de Lamballe who pulled from his chest, before expiring, the arrow that had pierced his heart. Iwerzon his two legs broken, fell, crushed under the feet of the horses. Remendall had his head cut with a back handed sword stroke. Krouadur was torn apart by two barbarians who cut up his body as if he were a stag. Morzol was caught by the hair to the tail of a horse and cut to pieces by axes. Pesked and Ker-Noaz were crushed by the chariot wheels of King Kenric. This last, of gigantic height, surrounded by ten colossi, stripped to the waist, who passed him arrows, stood at the front of his chariot, drawing back an immense bow the height of a man, and terribly ravaged the last defenders of King Arthur.

Protected by their breastplates, Maret de la Roche and Driant de la Forest still defended their king with desperate fury. Mordred, held back by the last phalanxes of the *Cornwall*, had not yet been able to get near his father, at whom he swore through the mêlée.

"I want to see your blood," he cried, "the cursed blood that brought me to birth."

Adragante, at last back near Merlin, had retreated behind a rock from which he fired his last arrows while awaiting his death.

It was Mordred, through a gap in the fight, was the first to see the druid and his disciple.

"So there you are," he sniggered, "fine holy chanter, bastard of gods and whores. I was looking to settle your account. Where are your fine knights now? Ha! The Round Table is empty, it seems to me. And it is I who will drink their blood from the emerald cup. Come dog, recommend your soul to the decrepit ancestor who sits in the clouds of your brain. I will send you to sup at a table in hell at the same time as your dear Adragante."

As he said this he threw his javelin at the head of Adragante the Gaël, but the mage, concentrating all his force, diverted the weapon in midflight before it reached his disciple.

At this astonishing superhuman act, Mordred blanched, hesitating a second.

"You can have your spear back, and for ever," cried Merlin, fixing the felon with eyes of fire. "I will escort you to the kingdom of toads, where you can start your life of expiation. Be cursed, cursed, cursed!"

Mordred tried to raise his shield, but paralysed by the power of the magus, was incapable of a saving reflex.

The javelin thrown back by Merlin struck him between the eyes, under the visor of his helmet. He wobbled in his saddle, beat the air with his hands, and slid heavily to the ground.

Merlin looked at his hand with a shudder, and recalled the imprecations of the druidess. He had given him death.

"Mordred is no more," he whispered, without looking at Adragante, "let us get closer to the king."

Merlin knew that the death of the traitor could not prevent destiny from being accomplished. And despite the confusion that suddenly swept through the enemy army, the bard saw King Kenric drive his chariot towards Arthur to avenge his ally.

The last bodyguards fell. Driant de la Forest expired under a Saxon axe. And Maret de la Roche, the swollen throat of the youth transfixed by an arrow, rolled spitting blood under the rearing horses of the standard bearers.

In a few minutes Arthur was surrounded by a group of enemy lieutenants. The terrible sword Escalibor turned toward the midst of the lances but the son of Uter-Pendragon was still threatened, and the magus was brusquely thrown back into the role of a warrior if he wanted to save his prince from death. A moment of pathos! At the same time that Merlin leaped to the help of the Prince he saw Kenric draw back his bow, and breaking an opening through the mêlée, send the fatal blow at the king whom the bards had claimed to be invulnerable.

Merlin seized a battle axe and struck it in Kenric's shoulder, who collapsed, reddening his chariot. Then clearing a way through the strident chaos with strokes of his sword where living and dead were mixed in a bloody mass, he arrived at the king to hold him in his arms.

Mortally wounded in the carotid artery, Arthur was at the point of death. The last two companions of the Round Table, Lucain and Gifflet de Fougères had recovered his sword, and the old warrior, whose eyes swam under already hollow eyelids, struggled weakly in the last spasms that announced the separation of the soul from the body.

His lips opened when he recognised the druid's face: "You remain the soul of Celtica," he murmured in a whisper. "Don't forget, Merlin. Britain… cannot… die. We… are the key… for the world! Farewell!"

"To the wagons!" cried Merlin, while Lucain and Gifflet dispersed the last assailants.

The Saxons, deprived of their two chiefs, began to beat a retreat to the north. Evening fell. The birds of prey already gathered in the pale sky where the first star shone. A frightful stench rose over the field of battle, mixed with the woody scent that the evening breeze carried from the edge of the forest. Beyond, the ebb tide of the Saxon army flowed in livid groups, leaving on the soiled ground the wreck of the low tide of battle.

Thousands of dead and wounded strewed the trodden ground, the humble wild flowers were crumpled in streams of clotted blood. All the confused remains, all the mutilated bodies, no longer belonging to one legion or another, all returned to the same cradle of sorrows, where tongues and races are abolished.

The evening hung its garlands of stars over the immense doleful field, and lives were extinguished one by one in a tumult of invisible souls. The great silence regained its rights. The peace giving virtue of moonbeams spread over the sinister plain, where Death at the gallop had harvested once more the tears of the world.

Here and there, human reptiles crawled again, trying to escape this Gehenna, the mouths of shadow demanding drink. Two or three pyres where the Saxons piled their dead were deployed on a horizon fringed with gold by great shrouds of flame.

The body of the king having been deposed in a covered wagon by Lucain and Gifflet, Merlin, who desired to regain the crest as quickly as possible, looked for Adragante the Gaël, who had disappeared.

"Adragante!" he cried anxiously in the darkness.

He continued to call several times, seeking the face of his disciple among all those lying in the growing darkness.

"Adragante, my son," he cried again. "Where are you?"

A form rose slowly in the shadows, its hair sparse and matted with blood, the torso stripped, the chest gashed with a frightful wound. What was this silent and tottering spectre?

"Is that you, Adragante?" asked the magus.

"Yes, it's me," responded the child with a moan.

Merlin could not repress a cry of horror. In a flash he heard the predictions of the Pontiff and of Sklera. This cursed day among all consummated his ruin and his defeat. It was he, and he alone, who had transformed this adolescent, full of youth and beauty, into a tottering phantom that seemed already to have found its tomb. He had an urge to break his lyre and trample on it before this innocent victim he had sent to the grave.

But Adragante had fallen back to the ground, and the bard, forgetting all, threw himself upon him, taking the bloody corpse in his arms and carrying it to a wagon, lit now with a miserable lantern. Alas! When he had laid him on the straw, near the remains of his king, Adragante the Gaël was no more than a corpse.

Merlin, his eyes dilated, his face tense, for the first time in his life was overcome by a suffering that was greater than himself. He could not drag his eyes away from these two bodies; the royal ancestor, the invincible hero, who for three quarters of a century had made the West tremble, and this knight in the flower of youth, the youngest and last companion at the feast of the Round Table. Between these two poles, the old man and the child, all the void of the massacre.

However, night had now fallen. It was necessary to strike camp and flee forever from this plain of misfortune. Merlin assembled the last survivors of the army, and placed them under the command of Lucain and Gifflet de Fougères. He asked them to give him the king's sword, the valiant Escalibor, that had never left the belt of the Prince. Then he gave the order to prepare the wagons to depart and gain the coast more quickly.

"Don't worry any more about me," he told them, "nor of the sacred load of which I take charge. Give me a knight to drive the wagon. I will leave alone with him. Join the *Cornwall* and the vessels that are moored before the Isle of Vecta. Set up emergency teams with the sailors who remained on board and the banks of rowers, and return to the land of Armorica."

The wagon trundled under the stars across woods and fields. Before the team of white oxen, whose bloodied shafts still carried the traces of the mêlée, the bard went at the pace of his horse, escorting the phantom wagon, the 'carriguel Ankou' of Celtic legend, that squeaked in the age old ruts of the hollow ways, jolting toward the unknown.

His hand on the king's sword, the twice defeated Merlin hung his head. In being present at the wreck of chivalry he began to conclude a chapter of his life. He was no more the warrior bard of the now useless harp. If he decided to live on the margins and, far from men, reconstruct an arch of alliance and love, who could stop him from attempting the supreme experience?

A great debate began in his heart. He was baptised, marked with the seal of the Christians. The Pontiff had assured him so. He had received the message of the Crucified and the secret of Joseph of Arimathea. But the Enchanter of the forest still had too much pagan blood in his veins to *resign* himself to the disaster that he had countersigned and sent those he loved to a problematic future life…

Why not fight against the brutal fact of death? Why not perform again the descent of Orpheus into the inferior shadows? Had they not said that the wonder worker of the East had declared 'his kingdom was not of this world' and yet had recalled the dead to life simply because they were his friends?

But how best to resuscitate these beings, thought Merlin, if life truly was only a tissue of misfortunes? Yet the resurrection of the dead appeared, even to the Essene, as the miracle of miracles. Life thus remained a treasure and the greatest of all!

A shudder ran through Merlin at the hope of a possible resurrection of Arthur and Adragante. He had certainly, since he had soaked his hands in blood in the course of the accursed battle, ruined his prowess as a mage. But there remained the faeries the Pontiff of the Neimheid had formally promised for his help. *If* however! Magus or Christian? The moment had come to choose.

Merlin drew up his horse. Over there in the moonlight he saw breaking like fleecy clouds the leaves of the immense Gallic forest. A supernatural force had passed in the direction of the arboreal sanctuary. To his right shone the waters of a lake, guarded by poplars like a cordon of watchers.

Having given the order for the driver to wait, Merlin got off his horse and went alone to the edge of the dark waters. Seizing the king's sword, he took it from its scabbard and raised the blade to the sky.

"Stilled is the hand of the prince who held you in combat! Closed are the spangled eyes the colour of the sea! Cold is the heart that beat only for his country. No hand any more is worthy to take you from your scabbard. You have never failed in honour. Marvellous sword of the king, predestined to retrieve alone from the stone, before the assembly of armed men! Farewell! Go to your last sleep in the deep waters under the chalice of water lilies!"

And taking in both hands the heavy sword by the hilt he threw it into the midst of the waters.

A column of foam spurted up, as if from the depths of the lake, then subsided as spray in dazzling sparkles. At the same moment, a mysterious hand came up from the waters, and brandished Arthur's sword. Three times the gesture was repeated, then the hand disappeared, the agitated waves calmed, and the lake slept once more under the stars.

At this sign the bard understood that all was not lost. All the spells, all the enchantments of earth and sky awaited him, if he consented to perform an act!

He gave in. He went back to the wagon where the two bodies lay, and taking the silver horn that the patriarch had given him, turned to the forest and sounded the call to ask the help of the druids.

The call echoed long into the night. Then, from afar, Merlin perceived the response from the sanctuary. "The spell is cast!"

"Take my horse," said the mage to the driver of the wagon, "and leave me now. Rejoin Lucain and the rest of the army. You will arrive soon enough to embark on the *Cornwall*."

The knight obeyed. He mounted the horse while Merlin held the reins and sadly stroked its neck. So many memories were attached to this marvellous beast that had never been ridden by anyone but him. But it was necessary to part. He needed, above all, a courier to take his last message across the land.

"What should I say to the chief of the detachment?" asked the knight. "When are you coming back to Armorica?"

"You can tell the knights that I will only return to the land of Brittany to take refuge in the forest of Broceliande, which I will not leave again. Now listen to me. Our king is not dead. He sleeps in the wagon. He sleeps – hear me well – beside Adragante. Have that message passed on, from Merlin to Lucain and Gifflet, so that they repeat it, on disembarking, to all the Bretons of Armorica:

"We were vanquished at Salisbury, but KING ARTHUR IS NOT DEAD!"

✢ ✢ ✢

PART TWO

PRELUDE

1 God, give me your strength, and in that Strength, the courage to suffer – to suffer for Truth – and in the Truth complete light – and in the light the whole of Gwynfyd* – and in the Gwynfyd, Love – and in Love, God – and in God, the absolute Good.

2 Today, feast of Alban and of solar fire, solstice of the new summer, I, Adragante the Gaël, last disciple of Merlin, the Sage of Sages, begin this writing with letters that we were given by the notches on trees, and by the notches on branches of trees from the temple of Broceliande.

3 May Menw,** the son of three cries, shower me at the fountain of light that the Father of all things, whose name cannot be revealed, will inspire his most humble Gwyddoniaid,† charged to guard the store of sayings, and dare to transmit it in writing to the posterity of the Kymrys.

4 Of the Kymrys who wandered in countries oversea, to the confines of the beautiful Tapobrane, land of eternal spring, and who, after many migrations, came to the Isle of Britain, that none living had struck with their prow before, and there implanted the race of lion hearted men.

5 And who, later, in the reign of King Arthur, driven by pirates come from the north, passed the emerald straits again, and established themselves on the coasts of Armorica, where the heart of the sea beats endlessly.

6 May the Almighty who reigns over Broceliande and the green and blue sea that strikes the shores of Armor and Argoat,†† give me the

*	Circle of Bliss	†	Druid
**	Hero and enchanter	††	Brittany

strength to give witness. For this is a witness of the truth moving in all its ways, like the green and blue sea, but unique in its essence like the sea. May the Lord of the legions of stars, the Master of the Sky and the Milky Way, luminary and country of delivered souls inspire me!

7 May the day come without evening when death will be banished, and where in the great circle of the creation of essences, three things will prevail for ever: Fire, Truth, Life.

8 For the torch of the sun will only be extinguished in the abyss to be reborn in another world, at the transformation of our eyes of sand. For the light of truth will only be obscured in some souls to break more intensely in others. For the flame of life only appears to be extinguished, and is renewed in new dawns of transmigration, to go and find ourselves one day in the crimson circle of Gwynfyd.

9 God, give me your Strength, and in that Strength the courage to suffer – to suffer for Truth – and in the Truth to find all light – and in my light – Life, Fire, Truth – the true, the beautiful and the divine. Amen!

I

This is a witness given to the most wise Merlin, who lived at the court of King Arthur, in the Isle of Britain and in Armorica. Merlin the bard with the golden torque who sang to his lyre and became the white druid of the forest of Broceliande.

At that time, Arthur, King of Britain, had driven off the Saxons and fought against the barbarians. And Merlin, who sat on the right of his throne protected him in his combats, and sang at his side the bardic chant of the Invincible. But a day came of the fault of the king, and the fault engendered a felony, and from the felony was born defeat.

Salisbury! Salisbury! Plain of desolation haunted by vultures. The blood that bathed your clay and your moss has not yet dried, and the bones of my brothers, wanted only by the wolves and birds of prey, still whiten in the arena where, more than half a century ago, the Bretons and Saxons cut each other's throats until the rising of the moon.

Until the rising of the moon the Knights of the Round Table fought around King Arthur, against the warriors of the traitor Mordred, and the reinforcements of Kenric, the Saxon king, which decided the end of the battle. Thus perished the flower of the Knights, under the unfurling sea of barbarians. Thus fell King Arthur, when the first star shone.

But chivalry, founded by the wise Merlin to perpetuate the tradition of honour, is not dead. Other companions took their place at the Round Table, dubbed by the shadows of those who were no more. The cup of friendship circled from mouth to mouth, with the secret of knighthood, so that the grape vines will blossom on the hills on the side of the sun, and the corn will ripen under the caress of summer. The seed of truth, the divine cereal, will pass from master to disciple, and souls will germinate each other until the final reintegration.

Chivalry is not dead, any more than King Arthur. For the night that followed the defeat of the army of the Celts, the King was transported by Merlin to the Neimheid, where the Great Pontiff of the Isle of Britain sits. Cared for by the ovates, he was saved from death, and taken by Barynthus the ferryman to the Isle of Avalon where the sun sets.

And Merlin took Escalibor, the king's sword that had never failed, and threw it in the waters. And a hand brandished it three times, like a farewell and a promise. And a voice was heard descending from the stars to the surface of the waters, which said "King Arthur is not dead!"

King Arthur is not dead. Guarded by faeries, he sleeps in a grotto of black marble on the Isle of Avalon, in the far West, where the sun sets. The faeries watch over his sleep, and await the hour of his awakening, to the voice of the bards, and the deliverance of all the Britons.

King Arthur was saved by Merlin the night following the defeat at Salisbury. And I, Adragante the Gaël, on that same mysterious night, when I had my chest torn open by a Saxon spear, and where I was already on the shore of shadows, was recalled to life by my Master.

And when I returned to life, in the lights of the Neimheid, Merlin's sparkling gaze was fixed upon my face. He put a finger to his lips, and took my hand. And I saw that I had no wounds. And we went forth into the blue night under a garden suspended from the stars. And we walked a long time in silence until we had reached the shore of the sea.

And there Merlin said to me: "Adragante, my son, you who were already born a second time by the divine word, are here also born again to earthly life."

And as I was about to reply I was astonished to find that no sound came from my mouth. The Sage said to me: "Adragante, you are the son of the secret, and because you have been resuscitated you will be dumb in this second life. You will see, you will hear, you will smell, you will feel, but the black god has sealed your mouth, and you will no longer give witness by word of mouth."

I made another attempt to speak, but in vain. And my eyes filled with tears.

And Merlin wept too.

"I had need of you," he told me. "And to bring you back from death I had to appeal to the Pontiff of the Neimheid, to forget the message of the martyr-god, and make a new pact with the god-force.

"I do not know whether you would rather be here, in the circle of transmigrations, but you have become, through my will, the son of my desire and of my thoughts. It is no more exactly you that lives, but my soul that lives in yours. And perhaps one day you, the child of silence, when you have seen and heard, will bear witness in writing. As God wills. And that the holy will be accomplished."

And as the Master read something like regret in my face, he said: "The regret you feel and that I express for you is my own regret; that of all the sons of heaven whose basic regret is to live down here ever unfulfilled. From now on you and I are the same lone soul, and the forest will be our refuge."

The mage then took his harp and raised it in the air before the sea, where the regular waves breaking on the sand of the beach sounded like a distant cymbal, and proclaimed, his face turned toward the stars:

Stars, my sisters, listen to my swan's song
On the golden harp I have for long sung
The great deeds of the old Britain, my country
When the banner of Arthur floated over the West!

But one day has sufficed for a kingdom to fall.
The banner of Arthur has slid in blood.
The plain of Camlan is no more than a gulf of shadows.
The bones of the dead whiten under the moon.

Deserted the palace, empty the Round Table,
And my harp has sung the last lai of death.
Farewell my knights, farewell my young shadows
Never more will the bard with the golden torque sing.

Stars, my sisters, this is my swan's song.
Hear the last lai on the golden harp,
Before it goes to sleep in the midst of you
Dumb as the night and as Adragante.

But Arthur, King Arthur is not dead!
On the Isle of Avalon where the sun sets,
In the marble tomb guarded by fays,
He sleeps waiting the dawn of the great awakening.

Rest, my king, brief will your sleep be;
Hoping for the call of the green country,
Like the sleeping lyre and the sword,
Rest waiting the call of the great awakening.

Merlin fell silent. The seven stars of the Great Bear shone over his tall silhouette. And we heard only the sound of the mounting sea.

Then the mage pointed in the direction of David's Chariot and added: "The body of King Arthur sleeps on the isle of Avalon, but his starry chariot is now on high. Pole star, immobile heart of the world, receive the royal charioteer who from now on will drive the starry quadriga across the fields of the firmament!"

73

For the last time Merlin caressed the seven strings of his lyre, and the rainbow harmony lit with its clarity the dark face of the sea.

And he threw his lyre into space and I saw that it stayed in the sky to form a brilliant constellation, on the edge of the Milky Way, between the Dragon and the Swan.

And the dawn appeared over the sea. And at a single stroke it chased away the people of the stars. And I saw, rapid on the waves, like a St Elmo's Fire, the hull of the pilot Barynthus, who came to summon us, my Master and me, to take us to the shores of Armorica.

And all the things I saw and heard, I, Adragante the Gaël, resuscitated by the most wise Merlin, and dumb forever, remained to bear witness. And this was written with a seagull's feather dipped in the ink of cuttlefish. And this writing, in praise of the Sublime Father and his beloved son, is my witness of Merlin, who took refuge in the woods after the defeat at Salisbury, and who became, in the mystery of the forests, the white druid of Broceliande.

II

I was now alone in my hut of dry leaves in the depths of the forest very close to a promontory overlooking the sea. On approaching Cape Fréhal the sage Merlin had left me, to accomplish the first part of his mission. We would only see each other again at the summer solstice at the time of setting the hill fires ablaze to commemorate the solar light. He gave me his ring and his silver horn. Then after holding me in his arms he cut a branch of holly and set off, his hair streaming in the wind, as for some time I followed his figure, alternately seen in green shadow or bright sunlight, until he disappeared into the trees.

One by one the days passed from the sky. The fleece of their reopening darkened after the declining blaze at the zenith, and the blue bosom of the sea tensed with the first autumn winds. The forest reddened, the thickets thinned, the crows gathered over the pale September lakes. The tusked boars, the does with the white flanks of adolescence, those adorned with the ten horned candelabra, the diadem of the woods, crossed the yellowing clearings in leaping bevies. Wild dogs, wolves with fiery tongues, pursued them, whose victims in dire straits cried under the teeth of their executioners, while the setting sun rolled over the waves, dyeing with its bleeding entrails the bark of silver birch, the delicate armour of the faeries of the wood in the mature stillness of the forest.

Autumn, old autumn, season of first torches and the fall of the greenery, white flowing of the sky over the dead woods, poplars of old gold at the crest of the valley, sad swarms of leaves rushing in the north wind, lost beasts, volatile migrants, autumn, dear and poignant autumn, whose murmur of exile at times touched my heart.

I lived off spring water, fruits and wild berries. The approach of winter tormented me. I did not see a living soul, having only for companions the hosts of the forest and the birds in the sky.

Sometimes a ship passed on the open sea, light as a dream, towards the West, but I feared as much as desired its approach. With my infirmity, I was afraid of finding myself face to face with one of my fellow men.

Great harps of rain rayed the greyness of the skies. From columns of clouds in rout, galloping above the sea, leaden torrents devastated moor and dune, streaming in cataracts on the forest citadels now under open sky.

The animals were hidden, fleeing birds had deserted nature in ruins.

One night of storm, huddled in my hut, frozen to the bone, I lit with a flint the first broom fire, and called Merlin, raising my soul toward the Sublime Father to ask for help.

Had I been resuscitated only to endure new tortures and suffer a slow agony more cruel than the first?

Half dead with hunger and cold, I stretched out on my litter of dead leaves and wished to render up my soul.

I fell asleep, and then saw, for the first time, Merlin in a dream. He was of immense height, dressed as a Grand Master of the Druids, wearing the blue sash. Between his two hands, crossed on his chest, shone a bright star which beat like a living heart, and at each pulse projected a beam of brilliant light.

His voice seemed to come from the end of the world and his lips hardly moved, but I read his words in his eyes, transparent like rock crystal: "Adragante," he said, "why are you troubled? Have you forgotten the promise I made to watch over you, near or far, like the son of my soul? Three times already I have averted your death, without you knowing it. For humans do not realise the dangers they run, and that invisible hands divert them from their route. Your fate belongs to me, remember that, and that you are the apple of my eye."

These words comforted me. And I realised then that simple thoughts could relieve a purely physical distress.

Merlin continued. "Raise yourself from the constraints of your body. Accept only needs that are indispensable, and reduce their demands. I have given you two companions for your solitary life: Love and Hope. Merge yourself in the great universal soul, of which each thing you see will bring you its message. And know how to decipher the secrets of the world – in which you, as a human being, are a deep mirror.

"The more you free yourself from material demands, the more you will see clearly in the enigmatic book of the Universe. The test you are suffering at this moment seeks for its end to purify your heart. Soon the blind will see, soon, I tell you, the pig will have wings. When your soul has been weighed in the divine balance, you will understand things better. And when we see each other again at the Fire festival, you will no longer be yourself but a living and intelligent part of that sparkling wheel that turns the World. For the destiny of the Elect is to consume God and to be consumed. Yes, to burn with love while being consumed, like a candle.

"As for me, dear Adragante, my mission is accomplished by divine and mysterious metamorphoses. Thus the sacred oak loses its vesture of deciduous leaves in the autumn and is greened again at the breath of the sun of love. Thus the snake takes a new skin at the waning of the moon.

"I will shed little by little the skin of eloquence, the skin of ambition, the skin stained with blood and clay.

"And you, a solarian like me, and placed in the same zodiacal sign of the celestial Lion, will cross the same gulf of shadow, to find yourself one day in the natal light.

"Winter is coming and its rounds of silence. For moon after moon, you and I will know the exile of the wise in the drowsiness of frost-dimmed mirrors or may even find at our bedside the soothing murmur of life. The rustling of green palm leaves, the crystal tears of the lyre-case of the sky, the mysterious buzzing of gold and living dust, and all that will be no more. We will sleep like the grain in a storehouse of sparkling snow, and only the cries of the sea crows will cross the desert of our meditations and our dreams.

"May you be saved from the anguish of the solitudes! Be strong, Adragante, and do not forget the god who sleeps in your depths. One day soon he will awake, from an immemorial sleep, and the spark of the dawn will pierce through the shadows.

"Farewell. Tomorrow morning go down to the shore.

"You will thus know that I am near to you, and more vigilant than a bodily presence. I tell you this Adragante. You are down here as my witness, and my living self, and you cannot die… Farewell!"

He leaned towards me and touched my forehead, and I felt on and around me a supernatural warmth. A stream of sunlight ran in my veins, and all my flesh was like the burning wax of a torch.

I saw the Master disappear little by little, to retreat and mount vertically into the night. His robe enveloped him like a nebula as he merged with the starry dome, in which I now saw the shining constellation of the Lyre.

In the morning, having awoken, I went down to the beach as the Master had said. The storm had ceased, and the sea was calm and the colour of opal.

Under the promontory, a rock like a spear head, I found the body of a fisherman, his eyes already eaten by crabs. I took off his leather suit and put it on.

Less than a cable length away was his boat, and the sea on the ebb revealed its anchor in the sand.

A seagull came and sat on my shoulder. I stayed as still as a tree, restraining the beating of my heart, and I understood that this seagull was my brother of the sky.

I called in a low voice: 'Karantez' and at this name, its grey wings fluttered, and it flew gently to the boat, where it rested, looking at me with its agate eyes, as if it wanted to show me a sign.

I pulled the boat up onto the dry land and found it contained two oars, a harpoon and a net, full of silver fish. The cheerful seagull wheeled above my head, the shadow of the voyager coming and going, shining in the mirror of sand.

And then I felt that the Master was there. Dropping to my knees on the shore, before the rising sun, I gave thanks to the Lord of the sea and sky.

III

Winter passed like a shadow. The green and blue spring returned to Broceliande. The sparrow and the oriole sang in the perfumed pollen of the breeze, and the swifts deployed their triangular mass in the sky as if they were the legionaries of Camblan.

I saw Karantez again, my seagull with grey wings. He carried a starry narcissus in his beak, and stopping before my hut, dropped it on the threshold.

The land sang of love. The forest filled with a vast animal and vegetal murmur. The lace of the ferns surged on the humus of dead leaves, and the velvety primrose put her touches of light in a grass still spongy from winter.

Over toward the dunes, under the blue depths of the sky, I saw the mists of my country rising. My heart was seized with an inexpressible joy. I felt the universe penetrate me with all its seeds, and raise in the tree of my life the sap that I had thought dried up.

Several times I heard crystal laughter that reflected as echoes among the oaks. Distant songs came to my ears, filling my heart with nostalgia.

Here one afternoon I saw, in a clearing, nine young girls dancing in a ring among the anemones and buttercups. Their tresses of hair, resting on their snowy shoulders, ranged from wheat to ebony and their darling bodies were hardly covered by floating scarves. Seeing me, amid cries of surprise, they swiftly dispersed in a halo of crimson light.

The memory haunted me for several nights. And I felt in myself the needle of desire, thinking of these living fruits, honeysuckles of smooth and tender flesh, carnal hawthorn, thrilling roses swollen with blood, that the Creator had put in my path and that I had perhaps the right to pluck.

And I heard a woman's voice that said: "Sexual delight, queen of the nights; sexual delight, queen of the world, who does not know down here the mildness of your wings, who can support your dagger of fire?"

And I dreamed in my heart of the teachings of the wise Merlin and awaited a sign.

The following moon, I could not resist the desire to return to the sunny clearing and see the circle of faeries again. This time they did not vanish from my view. On the contrary, they became more friendly and looked at me. And one of them, having left the circle, came towards me, and without giving me time to take flight, wound her golden hair around my neck. And her two deep clear eyes were like gulfs of sea water, and I breathed her fragrance like a flower.

Then she leaned towards me and whispered in my ear, "I am Nivona, the faery of the hawthorn and moonbeams. When the pale star shines in the sky, and you cannot find sleep on your couch of dead leaves, call me in the secrecy of your being and I will come. And you will know such intoxication in my girl flower bosom that you will never forget me."

I was so troubled that I closed my eyes. And one by one the faeries of the forest came to brush against my face and tell me their name.

"I am Centaurée" said one, "the faery of grasses and dew drops. My arms are fresh as the dawn, and I weep tears so sweet in love that you would drink them like a liqueur and thus know the secret of my soul."

And another voice murmured, "I am Sanguine, the faery of crimson flowers and salamanders. My heart is starred with rubies and you would die to breath in the vapour of my blood."

And I heard, one by one, in a whirlwind of fragrance and warm breath, Azilis, the faery of mists and foams, whose hair is a magnetic mantle of love; Limosela, the faery of lakes, water lilies and dreams; Scabieuse, the faery of brambles and midnight stars; Mona, the faery of heather and farewells; Osmonda, the faery of barks and embraces; Lobélia, the faery of tamarisk and sheaths of mother of pearl; finally Belladone, the faery of poisonous substances and deceptions, whose eyes of black diamond give lethargy and her heavy crimson lips lunatic madness.

All pressed upon me, all embraced me. Their words fell on me like petals, and I felt obscure connivances with the corymbs of fragrant flesh that I inhaled with closed eyes, without moving or being able to respond, prisoner of my eternal silence.

From far off the sea breeze caressed the mane of the clouds, and all the perfumed pollens of woman and the forest seemed concentrated on my forehead.

The marjoram and the fraxinella, the sunflower and the tuberose, the hyssop and the gentian, the sea violet and the lavender, mixed their vegetal fragrance with those of hair, and my life, until then somnolent, suddenly awakened to the elation of nature in jubilation, and dreamed of plunging to the depths to melt in universal love.

Then having opened my eyes, and tendered my two arms, as if to draw to my heart all these sunny messengers, I saw no more. But at the centre of the clearing embraced by the fires of midday was a horsewoman, mounted on an alezane mare the hooves of which seemed hardly to touch the ground.

She was dressed in a sky blue robe which left her arms and shoulders bare. She wore heavy gold bangles at her ankles and wrists. On her forehead shone a star, and the two long plaits of her auburn hair struck against her breast. Her eyes, the colour of topaz, were like those of the ash grey crow, and her mouth in her face was like a scarlet wound. On her left fist she held an albatross, and above her head immobile sea swallows weaved a crown for her.

"I am Viviane," she said, "Queen of the Forest. No mortal has ever laid a hand on my virgin breast, and I contain in my perfect body all the enchantments of the earth. I am the snowdrop and the oleander, the forget-me-not and the wild marigold. I am a trove of precious stones, a bed of golden yellow flowers and *belles de nuit*, an orchard of round and downy fruits, a tree of fragile and powerful flesh where all the birds of the sky nest. And all the animals in the world palpitate in unison with my heart. I am a butt of faery sweetness, the star that all men adore without knowing it. I am the lover and the eternal mother, the old woman of cradles and tombs. I give life and death."

The vision lasted so long that I hardly had time to see the sun set, and at that same moment saw innumerable braziers alight on the crests of hills as on the evening of the *Cornwall* getting under way. The Korn-boud rang and rang in the distant heart of Broceliande and I recognised the feast of the Summer Solstice in the tongues of fire that rose to a star filled sky.

And Viviane, the Queen of the Forest, remained impassive on her mare, completely enmeshed in a network of flames.

Here now, along that extreme route that came from the sky, above the solemn growth of the oak trees, I saw Merlin appear, mounted on a black horse. This was no longer the druid. Indeed I could hardly recognise him, so rejuvenated did he appear. A doublet of dark velvet covered his shoulders upon which beat the wings of an albatross, a red dragon embroidered on his chest, a golden diadem around his forehead. He arrived at a gallop as far as Viviane, who gave flight to his albatross, and each of them stared. Then Merlin having come towards me, gave me the accolade, touched the ring he had given me and had me mount pillion behind him without saying a word.

And so it was that Viviane came to us! We galloped neck and neck across the maze of woods during which the late braziers were extinguished in the clearings of Broceliande. And we arrived at midnight at the foot of a crystal château, that rose under the stars at the edge of the ocean.

And I understood that it was Merlin himself who had led me by his will into the clearing of the faeries, and at the same time had chosen the rendezvous of the solstice for me to meet Viviane, the Queen of the forest of Armorica, with whom he was going to meet the test of woman and of love.

IV

At the end of an alley of gigantic oak trees whose opaque foliage obscured the light of day the rock crystal château rose on a cape overlooking the sea. Granite arches formed a walkway toward terraces built into the rock. Two glass towers, one to the east and one to the west, were capped with crenelations of malachite. The continuous sound of the four winds in the forest mixed with the murmur of the waves, and in the satin sky above the manor flew the sea birds of the ocean.

At the foot of the cape, before a door concealed in the rock which led to the castle by an underground passage, a schooner was moored night and day. In a creek of black and green water, protected from the sea winds by a cliff, this ship of Barynthus sometimes hoisted its sails and went off, riding the crest of the waves with the speed of a demon, carrying Merlin and Viviane.

Thus day after day the mage lived with the faery, to discover each other on the open sea, when the sun shone at its height, or in the privacy of the manor when the sky was covered with clouds.

Lone witness, dumb witness to the life of these two beings who had broken all links with the world, I saw them at dawn when the clouds of mist dispersed over the sea, and at evening when the oblique rays of the setting sun made this château of love into an immense transparent flaming emerald.

They were almost constantly immobile like two statues. They never approached each other. They never touched each other. I simply saw their lips move, and their hands raised slowly to draw a desire or a thought in the air. At moments their looks mutually pierced each other with extraordinary intensity.

Viviane was always dressed in white satin, her arms bare, her auburn hair retained at the front by a golden thread, then falling free to her shoulders. Merlin wore the black doublet of that first day, but retained the five pointed star to his throat.

Barynthus brought food, furniture, precious woods, vessels of gold and silver, heavy fabrics and shining silks. I prepared the table and served the Master and his companion. They lived on fruit, cereals and sea fish. One day Barynthus brought a roe deer that he had found dying in the forest, its throat pierced by an arrow. Merlin did not want to touch it but Viviane insisted it be served at table and ate it with pleasure. And her cheeks, usually pale, became flushed like the wine she drank from a scarlet aiguière. Then before me, the faery touched the hand of the mage, and they bit one after the other into the same sun coloured fruit.

That evening, which was in summer, I saw in the suspended garden, between the satin of the lilies and the velvet of the roses, a reptile glide of terrifying length. It made a sound of little bells as it slid over the fine sand, and then rearing up suddenly on its scaly stomach it shot its forked tongue in the direction of the manor.

Merlin and Viviane usually slept in two parallel twin beds without a canopy in the highest room of the western tower.

Through the glass ceiling they could see the sparkling people of the stars. And Merlin explained to his love the blazing life of the constellations, calling each golden point of the Milky Way by its name, and he showed on this background, in theorems of light, how each particle of the living creation is joined to the cosmic system. And the stars glided gently under their dreaming eyelids, and the celestial figures turned slowly, like a wheel, in the circle of immensity.

But that night, Merlin and Viviane were not sleeping in the highest room of the western tower. All the windows of the castle remained wide open, and the couple went onto the terrace bathed in moonlight, the balustrade of which overhung the sea. And I, pressed with a curiosity I had never felt before, went to sit on the flat rock that went down towards the beach – and I heard the words that fluttered through the silence of the night.

And Viviane said, "This night is so beautiful that I want to lose myself in it. The sea is so deep and blue that I would like to dissolve my white faery flesh in it. And your gaze is so beautiful Merlin, impregnated with moonlight, that I would like to plunge into its depths and stay there forever to know the depths of your soul."

And Merlin replied, "This evening, Viviane, your heart beats quicker than usual, for you are moved by the spirit of the Earth. The flesh of the animal and the blood of the red wine are before your faery eyes. And a desire as old as the world bends you under its yoke. Are you no longer the divine lover, the mirror of my soul, the well beloved that one weds with a single look? Have you become a temptress, the eternally tormented, the trickster of love who ceaselessly sets the divine cards at odds?"

And Viviane returned, "It is not cheating, my love, to follow one's destiny. The law of the world is love, and love means desire, and desire must be fulfilled. The gods themselves who engender in the alcoves of the clouds do not escape that law. All that lives down here carries the mark of sovereign desire. We, the faeries, are the daughters of love. We crystallise in our bodies of hot snow all the secret voluptuaries of loving nature. And you, the mage, are born like the others, from a kiss, from a spark of generating fire, and you carry in you, like an open book, the stigmata of that ineluctable law."

And Merlin responded, "Love as I see it has no need of these carnal sanctions. Nothing is more beautiful than the exchange of two souls, beyond the assuaging of the Beast."

And Viviane returned, "The Beast is divine, the Beast is sacred. It is man who has spoiled all with his sophistry. The act is nothing, you know very well. What counts is the thought behind it. And is there anything more beautiful than to recreate the divine act, by materialising one's love in the confection of a creature? Could a mage and a faery who come together create anything other than a hero or a son of heaven? I tell you Merlin, only love is sublime."

And Merlin responded, "In the beginning, no doubt, love was like that. When the creation had not yet been soiled by men. In the time when in certain species in nature the male died of joy in meeting the day. But today when the creation has been martyred, love, when it is not a simulacrum, only increases the disappointing chain of suffering and pain. What good is it to fall into the circle of generation and provide the death of new victims? All down here is only illusion, separation, immolation, sacrifice. Life and death go hand in hand and sorrow is so close to the voluptuous that these two daughters of creation seem drawn to the same gulf of agony, their cries, their masks and their furies..."

There was a silence, and then Viviane murmured, almost in a whisper, "Yes, I know... I know. It is the last argument of the sages who refuse to participate in the common life of the earth. They put their pride before all. They take no account that they act thus because they are afraid of life. And that this wisdom they recommend is, at base, egoism and cowardice. And I repeat to you from my faery mouth. To love, to be loved, to burn, to be burnt, that is the eternal law of couples. And so much the better that with disenchantment and nostalgia they must pay for the act that, for a few seconds, makes them feel like God!"

I heard a sigh in the shadows, and something like the beating of wings. All appeared to me, in the milky clarity of midnight, as veiled with resignation before the infinite bitterness of all things. The sea accepted its convulsions, the earth its wounds, all creation its vertiginous range of sorrows. And the silence of Merlin, that came to trouble the emanation of a faery, ratified the fatality of suffering that hung over the universe.

Again Viviane began to speak softly, and I, Adragante the Dumb, trembled at each of her words. As if the words pronounced by this tepid shadowy mouth, with the wet lips of the moon, recovered their original significance.

"Merlin, my sweet friend," she said, "do you not believe that our eyes have been made to be showered with light and colour? Our nostrils to breathe in and breathe out all the perfumes of the world? The shells of our ears to echo the vibrations, the music and the whole ocean of symphony that plays the wind and man on the lyre of the universe? That all the organs of our body have their purpose and the desire for their purpose. And to refuse one of them the right to express itself is to martyr creation, to repeat your words just now. All thirst, on this earth, must be quenched. The thirst for love, more than the others, because it partakes of the mysteries of creation. Merlin my sweet friend, drink to your desire, sate your desire to the point of sating your whole being, and accept that most sweet slavery here in the arms of a faery. Accept, without holding back, the return to the living cradle. The crossing of the crimson straits in the ship of my body of dream…"

I heard a hissing in the night. And again I saw the serpent, that slid slowly between the rocks, and stretched its flat head toward the bed of sleeping flowers. And I felt what was woven in this same shadow of immemorial nights, the same legend of love as that of ancient days, the same plot of love that ceaselessly undid and redid the tapestry of the Mother Goddess. And a cloud of silver veiled the immaculate disc of the moon, while I heard a sound of crumpled silk, a sound of material falling, and a moan of love responding to the smothered prelude of a nightingale intoxicated with stars…

V

On that same night, I saw prodigies in the sky and across the sea. The château of rock crystal seemed to mount into the air like a diamond pyramid, and in the central facet I saw a naked woman with closed eyes surrounded by a cloak of flames. I recognised Viviane. On her head a black and white sea eagle with immense wings was perched, that had the eyes of Merlin and carried at its crop a shining star. The Lyre vibrated in space, and the constellations became human faces and forms, while the moon raised its mask of frost to show the mysteries of its starry flesh.

And each star spoke in turn. And it was the voice of Merlin that resonated in space, to the harmonies of the firmament with his lyre. And I heard the sound of bells and organs rising from the heart of the sea.

"We are the wandering stars," said the planets. "We take charge of the destinies of those who are born in our shadow, and guide them from the womb of their mother to the womb of the earth. We are the stardust, particles of the great Fire of love in ancient times – of the eternal sun of love that moves the wheel of the world. It is we who ignite the desire for birth, and to love and reproduce, in the veins of the sleeping, in the roots of plants, in the shadowy kingdom of mines and springs. We are the torches of the temple, the lights that have burned since the beginning of the world before the Master of the infinite light."

And the moon said: "I am the Eternal Feminine, the multiform spouse of the Sun god. I am the face of desire that burns in the shadows; the magnetic source of all desires. The tides of the sea and the blood of woman receive their irresistible rhythm from me, and the heart of the earth submits to my laws. Phoebe growing from the penumbras, Selene, princess of the new, Tanith or Hecate, I am the silver cup of births, and the shears that cut the thread of destinies. The love I dispense to its seed of death. I make the wine ferment, seed the poisonous plants, and fertilise the sepulchres. I am the dial of the agony and I sign the foreheads of corpses. My waning is deathlike and I glean from the shadows. Water plants belong to me, water lilies, white lilies and dead leaves. The palm tree extends a root at each hour of my light, and it is from my rays that the new born spring forth."

And Mars, projecting his ruddy stain on the night, said in his turn, through the voice of Merlin: "I am the planet of combat and violence. Fire of conflagrations and the heart of man, tongue of wild beasts and spurt of wounds, I am anger and rape, the flaming dragon of heroism and spasm. In my flanks murdering and healing metals are found, and I pour passion in the hearts of the strong. Vultures and wolves haunt my hills where euphorbia and nettles grow. I rule alternatively the Ram and Scorpion, and the South-East winds."

And a hardly visible star in the hollow of the night grew suddenly, and dominated with its light all the other constellations. "I am Jupiter," she began, "the blue star of glory and serene joy. I represent in the sky the material emanation of the Sublime Father. I am the Archer of the celestial forests where the sacred animals of the zodiac abound. The oak and the olive are my blessed trees. I am radiant and magnificent. The royal eagle and the seagull live in my clouds, and in my right hand, adorned with an immense sapphire, I hold the keys of happiness."

"And I bring misfortune," replied a vast ghost planet with a luminous ring suspended in the sky. "I am Saturn the Obscure, father of autumn and decline, the much loved star of black magicians. My colour is lead and metallic black. I am hardship, opposition and abortion. It is I the constellational gouty, the morose patriarch with the hourglass of long and sombre destinies. My thin and pale nakedness presides over caverns, deep lakes, empty lands, dark and stinking cess pits. I am the usurer of eternity, the contemplator of pale infinities. My talisman preserves against lethargies and premature burials. They consecrate me with perfumes of sulphur and scammony. I am the god of the cypress and black hellebore, the toad of the rocks and the cuttlefish of the shores. I dig the graves of my lovers. I arouse the sadness that follows carnal satisfaction. My gaze is the ash heap of all earthly joy."

And from all this sequined multitude who appeared in the amphitheatre of the night, I saw emerge successively the sons and daughters of the sky who told me their name, their destiny, and the mysterious links that attach them to us through the astral light.

The Ship at the start of the Milky Way which puts the cap on the Unicorn where the placenta of faeries is formed; Sirius, the golden country, chrysolite of the shadows that haunts the alchemists' athenors; the tetragram of Orion, whose heart is a starry pentacle in the open sky. The Grape Picker, on the right arm of the Virgin, who presides over the wine press and the presses of blood; Antares, at the heart of the Scorpion, who pierces the hearts of knights in love, and causes the spider of the tombs to flourish; the Fish of the North and the Fish of the South, joined by a ribbon of stars, the first swallowing Andromeda, the second pointing to the square of Pegasus, natal ether of poets and chimeras; the Hare and the Dove, the Eagle and Dolphin, all this heavenly paradise where the animals of the golden age were petrified by the gods into stellar hieroglyphs. And in the middle of this scintillating round of night like the pulsation of a divine body, the Pole Star rested immobile at the centre, the star of the North and the old Hyperborean dream, that marks the heart of the world. And as the night advanced each star resumed its rank and its itinerary in the promenade of moon dust.

And then, with the voice of Viviane, rising fresh and sweet, I saw a scarlet star, a naked red star, that opened its calyx over the sea.

And this star told me: "I am Venus, the most mysterious Morning Star. My heart is dual, for under the name of Lucifer I rise in the east at break of day, and under the name of Vesper, I announce from the west the falling of night. I am the radiant, the pure, the saint of dawns and the faery of evenings. I carry in my breast all the loves of the world. I am the mirror of wisdom and divine lust. In me are hidden the past, present and future goddesses, and I burn like a jewel of fire on the hand of the Sublime Father. About me fly the turtle dove and the dove. My magic herb is vervain and I who preside over sacred mysteries. I am the wife and the lover, the mother and eternal nature. There is nothing living that has not passed through the tabernacle of my holy womb, that holds all the seeds of the future. I am Viviane the Opener, the daughter of forests and torrents, the shell of flesh coming out of the foam, where I was shaped by the hand of the gods!"

And a last star shone in the sky that I recognised as the flamboyant star suspended from the throat of Merlin, and in the heart of this star I recognised the human image of my master. A diadem of fire shone on his forehead. A golden halo surrounded his face. His eyes were like those of an eagle who speeds toward the sun. In his right hand he held a lyre and in his left a book, and a sword hung at his belt.

And he said: "I am the companion of Venus. At sunset and at dawn I am the golden lamp with its star of love. Son of the Sun moulded from the dust of the earth, Ithyphallic through the nuptial mystery, I light the torch of the hymen in the bed of the sleeping goddess. I am the solar intelligence, the idea-force seeding dark and rebellious matter, the bearer of the caduceus. My name is Mercury. Poet and divine, God of the stealers of fire, conductor of souls, inventor of writing, lord of music and the divine word, I am the hermaphrodite, the universal instinct of creation, the son of Maia, perpetual tearer apart of the illusions of heaven and earth. The swiftest of stars, I approach the Sun. I symbolise infancy and its vitality. I have no colour. I am the prism of the rainbow. I refract all things, that which is high and that which is low. I am the secret fire, the convertible mediator, indifferent to good or bad, the plastic and imaginative soul of the world, the dragon of the astral light. The Wind has carried me in its belly, the Earth is my wet-nurse, it is I, the Trismegistus, father of the Emerald Tablet.

"And now here. I have undergone the test of love. I have burnt the flesh in love. I have crossed the mortal seductions of love. In God I have found strength – and in that strength the courage for suffering – suffering for truth – and in that truth I have found my Light and my Love."

And the voice ceased in the immensity. And all the stars went out, apart from Mercury and Venus. And Merlin fused again with Mercury. And Mercury became the diamond château. And the château dropped into the luminous calyx of Venus. And Venus herself went out. And I saw nothing more but the infinity of the sea… and heard no more but the infinite sound of the sea.

VI

The next day I awoke in the lower house which was already golden in the first rays of the summer sun. The grass was still diamonded with the dew of night, and over the thick foliage of the forest the sky spread like a great blue bird. I left, and Karantez the seagull came towards me, his shadow covered my shoulders as he perched on my head fluttering his wings. Merlin's château shone in the rising sun. And I did not know if I had been the mere toy of a dream.

But here on this joyful morning, descending the gulf, I saw the two masted ship of Barynthus, who put up his great russet sail, and sped over the sparkling mirror of the sea. Viviane was alone on the bridge, in her robe of white silk, waving her hand in the direction of the shore.

Then on the balustrade of the castle, where I was about to climb, I saw the Master in his druid robes, just as he had appeared at the feasts of the Round Table. His face was distant – as if never delivered to any earthly desire. Immobile, his fists clenched on the granite support, he seemed to ignore the ship of Barynthus on the brilliant mirror of the sea.

When the boat that carried Viviane had passed the cape and gained the open sea, the Master opened his left hand, and I saw a drop of water trembling in his palm. And this drop of living water, which the sun respected by not absorbing it, had the transparency of the sea.

And Merlin said to me, "This is a tear of Viviane, a fugitive dew that does not spare the face of faeries, and which condenses in a farewell to the pleasures and regrets of love."

He touched Viviane's tear with his right hand and it instantly solidified. Then he held it between his thumb and index finger, at the level of the horizon, where the ship was no more than an imperceptible point, and said: "With this little tear I abolish the vision of the ship. Now that I have known love, so that no nostalgia for the unknown can ever torment my heart, this tear will eternalise my power as a mage. For with it I efface, on the frontier of their passing, faery, ship, and love."

I then saw that the horizon was empty, and that the visible gulf of the present had removed from our regard something that was already no more than a memory.

And Merlin, having taken the tear of the faery, placed it in the five pointed star, saying: "This is farewell. This may seem death to all men who believe only in the omnipotence of matter. It is only necessary for me to *really* follow that voyage, while leaving my body in the crystal château. But the sun of love that opens out the world is too great for our mortal hearts, and we represent a divine mirror as broken pieces that only reflect fragments of heaven.

"What are we, Adragante? Physically like sponges, quickly saturated, on which all the waves of the Ocean could surge without being able to add a drop. Moral abysses, no multiplication of which could fill the infinite. Men and women who seek to possess each other without having the power to unite, even at the sublime moment of creative explosion. Who represent metaphysically the impossible fusion of unity with zero. The giddiness of love surpasses the act in which it has an end. It breaks through the carnal to inundate the soul. The only real possession can be held in a glance. The world is given to he who knows and wills. He brings to birth by the Word."

Merlin passed a hand across his lips as if to efface any trace of the kisses of Viviane.

"It matters little," he said, lowering his voice, "that over there on the sea, a faery, whose bodily splendour could trouble the angels, carries in her heart the seed of my mortal desire! The lines of blood are more hazardous than those of thought. And should I repeat a thousand times the blind act of the flesh, I can only subdivide myself and perhaps uselessly complicate the shadowy maze of creation. For a thousand nights of love are only innumerable facets of a single and same embrace. Cosmic love and desire held in its kiss, like the pain and regret of the world, resides in this single tear, fallen from the eyes of the Enchantress."

Merlin turned towards me and looked deeply into my eyes, putting his hands on my shoulders. "The time has come, Adragante, when I must lose a part of my magnetic force. The faery will return, I know, for new tests. But the short space of life somewhat limits the time given me to accomplish, with your help, the rest of my mission. Prepare yourself for strange journeys. And be surprised at nothing. Be my obedient disciple. After this dawn of solitude the great lesson of the world will begin for us, of the eternal conflict of all things, without mercy or pity, which divides princes of the blood from slaves, and puts two races in permanent rivalry, the titans and the gods. And now, follow me!"

Merlin, going before me, marched toward the crystal château. We climbed the flights of stairs and entered the magic house where the perfume of the faery still drifted.

Three long halls, paved with black and white marble squares, decorated with animal skins, precious cloths and musical instruments, stretched one after the other to an immense oak double door guarded by two groups of animals on plinths, sculpted in granite. To the left a bear, to the right a wild sow suckling its young. On the left hand leaf of the door an apple tree was carved, enlaced with gold. On the right hand a flower with three branches.

The Master went to the group of sucklings and put his hand on the neck of the sow. "My son," he said, "this sow can teach us a lesson. She is the mother of all, the omnifecund. She gives the milk of courage, invisible strength and tenacity, intrepidness to all tests. As you already know, the boar is the national and religious emblem of the Bretons, because it never flees, because it refuses immolation, and because, with its giant snout it faces up to the pack. It is our symbol and our totem, and it is good that it also represents the monster of the storm and the polar animal, whose final destiny is to be vanquished by the solar bear. An image of the struggle that opposes the powers of primordial instinct and the sovereignty of intelligence. Remember the hunt of our King Arthur (the royal bear) who after nine days and nine nights ended by defeating the wild boar. Both are seen in and comprise the constellation of the Wain that shines in the North, over the sea."

Merlin then approached the door and touched with his finger the image of the apple tree. "This is the apple tree of the Isle of Avalon, the sacred tree of the ancestor of the Celts, of which each fruit carries the pentagram of Knowledge at its core. It is the number of the star of the west, the 5, in rivalry to the 6 of the east, which three times repeated gives the mark of the Beast."

"Finally," said Merlin, indicating the flower, "here is the most mysterious symbol of the Graal – the *magical* name of which can never be uttered when the ceremonial cup is passed at the banquets of our Knighthood, but with which I wanted, all the same, to mark on the forehead of the troops, like a saving invocation, before the battle of Salisbury. The blood of the wounded god – which god? – spilled by the lance of the soldier or the snout of the sacred beast, sinks into the earth and gives birth to a flower. Which flower? Over there, where the sun rises, the lotus. Here, where the sun sets, the rose or the water lily. The god changes name but is ever the same."

Merlin put his finger to his lips. "The Almighty, the Sublime Father, of whom no one, not even the Pontiff, knows the true Name."

Merlin now went over to an oak chest, and took from it a great leather bound book with steel clasps that he put on a table between two silver candlesticks.

"You do not know, my child," he told me, "that in the druid colleges there is a tradition never to write. That is to say, the holy Word must be passed, like seed is thrown in the furrow, by the voice of adepts. In time to come, men overcome by their inventions will understand the dangers of written things; that can fall into unworthy hands and give place to lying interpretations, sources of passion and discord.

"Here," continued Merlin, opening the great book, "there is thus no written thing but a very Book of Wisdom in 78 images. You have before your eyes the testament of the winged god who guides souls and presides over the arcana of language. It contains the secret of the science of Numbers, and the hidden laws of the universe. God is a number, like you and me. Everything in creation acts by magic numbers. It is enough to learn for today that the number NINE is, above all, that of initiates and visionaries."

Merlin leafed through the book before my marvelling eyes. It was a collection of parchments, encrusted with precious materials, enhanced with striking colours. "The Book of Tarots," continued the Master, "is composed of 22 magic keys, which are the arcana of the essential doctrine, and constitute a hieroglyphic alphabet, where symbols are explained by numbers – and four decads, accompanied by four figures, each one marked with the signs of the sacred quaternity. In combining the arcana and the four signs, that one finds in all theogonies, the adept can discover the key to hidden things, the secrets of Life and Death.

"Here is the budding Staff, symbol of the male god. Here the feminine Cup that is also the flower of Isis, the flower of blood and the Royal Virgin; the most mysterious vessel of sacrifice, charged to recover the blood of the divine victim. It is the flower of three branches that you saw at that door, the most pure chalice of future oblations, where the transmutations of universal substance must be accomplished. Here is the Sword transfixing the Crown, symbol of entanglement and union, of which the image of the cross is the hieroglyphic sign. And then here, the fourth and last figure: a circle enclosing a lotus flower. That is the fruit of their union, the supreme creaturely sign.

"Each of these signs corresponds to one of the four letters of the unspeakable Name, and they resume in themselves the prodigious 'curriculum' of creation. I have told you of the number NINE. Look at the ninth key of the Tarot. It is the arcanum of the Hermit, the man of solitude, mine from now on, yours later, Adragante, when I am no more. We do not see like others. We know that the truth wounds us or freezes the heart. We plunge beyond daily life in the gulf of consequences. We are thrown over by others because we pass for prophets of disaster. But do we not look beyond the crack in the edifice, to the skeleton of the man who laughs, and in the banquet of joyful corruption to the next alignment of tombs?

"The number NINE – three times the Triad – is the most complete image of the three worlds, the reason for existence of all forms. You will note that the sow had nine sucklings, as there are nine druidesses

91

on the Isle of Sein, as it took nine days for our King Arthur to kill the legendary boar, as nine months is necessary for a mother to bring the new born into the world. Nine is the last and the greatest of the numbers expressed by a single figure. It divides and multiplies. 'NINE is ONE' say the Sènes, in their transports. NINE is the number of poetry, of the mystery, and of the TEST."

VII

Having opened the oaken door with a golden key hanging from his belt, Merlin signed for me to follow him. We found ourselves under a vault that gave on to a spiral staircase, lit here and there with naphtha lamps fixed to rock walls. We went down for a very long time. A coolness chilled our faces at the same time that an echo was reflected under the vault as we approached little by little what sounded like the continuous murmur of a torrent. After a time that seemed interminable we finally came out onto a dark platform where the roaring of the waters suddenly increased. We were in a grotto that I felt to be immense even though in the shadows I could see neither height nor depth.

"Be careful," Merlin said, lighting a resin torch from one of the naphtha lamps. "Walk in my footsteps. The undersea current is to the left at about thirty feet down. The way will become narrow and slippery, so hold on to my belt and guide yourself as best you can by the flame of the torch."

In the feeble light of his torch, I gradually distinguished the escarpments of a cavern, with deep and humid crevices and groups of rocks that in the shadows looked like sleeping giants.

By staring wide eyed, I thought I could distinguish at the top of certain narrow rocks sea birds of an excessive size. And on other flat topped rocks were naked women, whose wet and clinging hair clung to their bodies like bonds of captives, and whose gaze had the phosphorescent radiance of cats' eyes. As they watched me, it seemed, they slowly extended their arms, with reflections of scales, towards me. By the trembling movement of their lips I also believe that they cried or sang, but all was covered by the deafening cataract, which the height of the stone dome echoed to infinity.

At one point, I leaned over the dark gulf, that the wash of the current spattered with fugitive brightness, whilst a foaming column, as if forged from the rock, gushed salty sparkles as far as ourselves.

That odour, that taste could not deceive me. The water that surged in these places could only be sea water.

At the heart of the tumult I heard quite vaguely a kind of music, of bassoons, trumpets and strings, and there appeared other women with viscous bodies, whose hair seemed like octopus tentacles, and who presented themselves suddenly, breasts erect and stained with foam on their fin-like tails. Or fish that I took for leaping salmon, turning in a pattering network of spray, but my heart froze when I thought I saw the spotted scales and lance-like head of a marine monster.

My eyes becoming used to the dark, I noticed that the narrow path that Merlin followed turned around the gulf and that we were returning to the entrance of the cavern where the stone stairway ended and from which we would soon be separated by the immense column of the torrent; whose waters I concluded had just arrived in this bubbling ferment after many thousands of feet – for we had been walking for a very long time – and where myriad living creatures swarmed – that must flow from the bottom of an underground passage.

I entered, and felt myself now in a world whose reality had escaped me. That all was no more than a nebulous dream. "Am I dreaming?" I wondered. For despite my infirmity, I retained the power to form words within myself.

At that moment, as if Merlin wished to answer that question, he stopped at the edge of the torrent, and turning towards me, raised the torch above his head. He suddenly grew larger, and the star he wore at his throat began to flame like the sun. Then he pronounced some words I could not hear, and threw the torch into the midst of the gulf.

At that same moment the torrent stopped as if petrified. And the part of the cavern where we were was lit by the star that Merlin had taken in his right hand instead of the torch. The whole of life that surrounded us seemed suspended. And on the water that had became deep and transparent, foam and bodies coagulated into marble statues. And in this deathly silence I heard the Master speak almost in a whisper, as if in a temple.

"No, my son, you are not dreaming," he said, "but you are on the threshold of a mystery. To stop the course of things and of time is a terrible gift that was conferred on some immortals. And to begin one's immortality down here is to enter firmly into this state of superior perception, from which we learn that the dead are forever freed from time and movement, those illusions of our bodily senses. But since life is the antechamber of death, I have to show you this before entering into the tangle of forms and desires.

"What you see here is the matrix of the world, for man and his kingdom are born from the Ocean. And just as all seeding is in the image of the nebulae that gave birth to the suns, the same hermaphroditic womb that men call either the Ocean or the Sea contains the liquid seed of all things. But here, as in nature, the male god gives way to the mother goddess, the Virgin of salt and foam, who receives in her breast rivers and torrents, streams and fountains, and returns their essence in the clouds from which fresh water falls on our forests, to quench the thirst of the earth. Thus the bitterness of tears, Adragante, are transformed into life giving rain from which are born blood and milk, universal nourishment, the juice of the grape and the wheat of harvests."

While Merlin spoke, a shining light, as if supernatural, spread throughout the cavern. And I saw right at the end, at the far side of this marine lake, as great as the clearing of Arderidd, a group of menhirs of different heights, ranged against each other in the form of pyramids, the three last of colossal dimensions, rising to the arch of the vault. Between these three menhirs, disposed in a triangle, on the tops of which three milky white albatrosses were perched, there was a throne of stone, encrusted with shells. And on this throne sat one whom I recognised as the goddess of the place.

Her sun coloured hair was retained on the forehead by a silver diadem and revealed her ears, near which fish scales could be seen. Two sea serpents with birds' heads met over her head. She had a wing on each side of her forehead. Her eyes shone like two emeralds. Her hair passed under her arms and rejoined on her torso where only her navel and two breasts, with phosphorescent tips, could be seen. And on her lower stomach shone a star of the sea. And winding round her like tresses of leather, bunches of seaweed and gigantic stems of christes-marines rose as far as her thighs. She held up in her right hand a transparent chalice, in which bubbled the green blood of the sea. At her feet, on each side of her throne, two sirens were stretched out before shells of mother of pearl with iridescent cavities.

And on the basalt and granite rocks that descended to the water in tiers so regular that one would have thought them sculpted, unknown creatures were arranged, petrified by the hand of the Mage. Pygmies with the heads of seagulls; strange dwarves with beards of kelp at their fins, with backs like mackerel marked with the green and blue grooves of the sea; monsters with human faces and tentacles encrusted with precious stones; tritons with heads of turbot; sea horses with chests of youths, provided with arms and hands holding harpoons and nets;

jellyfish the colour of opals ending in a woman's body; shells with elastic and living flesh; giant mussels mounted on human feet, holding a tongue across a yawning mucus membrane; octopuses with children's eyes; squid with lions' manes; crustaceans with wolves' heads; limpets the colour of rust, winged like Lepidoptera; sea snails the colour of blood mounted on ithyphallic cacti; and all the half vegetable half mineral corals and madrepores. The three kingdoms were assembled, near the sea, in this fabulous cavern, with rock faces covered with sea wrack and moss, lichens and seaweed, all humid fleeces and somnolent moulds that engender movement and life.

Then I saw the goddess raise up her chalice from which a foaming vapour escaped. At this same moment the largest albatross flew from the menhir, slowly, as if in a dream, and perched on the throne of the goddess. I suddenly heard in the grotto a far noise that approached like a galloping horseman and I recognised the sound of the sea. And each being and each thing began to reanimate and wake up gently from a mineral sleep as the Master cried in a loud voice:

"I salute you, Onuava, three times holy, nourishing goddess through whom the world came to birth. You are the mirror of the infinite, the eternally desired, the wife of the sun god who bathes in your breast and whose breath animates and seeds your enormous body. Your sacred rages are terrible, but nothing is equal, when you calm down, to your sweetness and serenity, nor to the beauty of your sky coloured robe fringed with foam, which no mortal could ever soil, or tear the ever virgin silk. You are inviolable and immaculate, the breath of love and the scales of the world. O Mother of cosmogonies, in whom knowledge and wisdom are resumed, strength, and measure within that strength, show us the way to perfection. Preserve us, direct us, and protect the trees of the forest that go to sail upon your waves. And when our hour comes, make our death be gentle as the green depths, where our perishable forms return to be abolished in your empire that will have no end."

Thus spake the Master, in closing his hand on his star. And darkness took back possession of the cavern. I heard the torrent that gushed again against the rock, while the immense cavern echoed with the cries of the sirens, the innumerable rumblings of life coming to birth and the roaring of the sea.

VIII

Merlin took me by the hand and we walked through more corridors, descended more stairs – time no longer counted for me. I no longer knew whether it was day or night but I felt no fatigue or need of sleep.

We came to an underground hall, covered in a diaphanous and porous material, like the phengite stone of Cappadocia. And as the first grotto had been dark, so this one, where the day seemed to be enclosed, was full of bright light.

At the bottom of this square hall I saw a high granite chimney, in which a strange fire burnt with upright blue flames, tended by two gnomes who disappeared at our arrival.

Here, over the fire, an earthen vase was being heated that had the form of a great hedgehog, surmounted by a neck of eight or nine inches, near which a glass egg was fitted where I saw a crimson material sparkling.

On one side of the chimney were stones and strips of lead. On the other, bowls were piled with emeralds, rubies, sapphires, turquoises and sardonix, diamonds of extraordinary size where lights of fire condensed, and ingots of gold shining like fragments of the sun.

And the Master said to me, "Here is the secret of Fire. Not the blind fire that destroys and calcines, and that men never know how to control, but divine fire, the fire of the wise, that presides over the birth of forms. For it is in obscurity and humidity, as you saw in the Temple of the Waters, that the mystery of birth is elaborated, but only the fire, to which the striving of inert matter belongs, can give it flight.

"Fire is the soul of the world. And no creature can emerge from chaos, arise and grow, without having been projected in the beginning, and specified by the arrow of fire. Fire, male and volatile principle, or sulphur, seeds the female and fixed principle with quicksilver, eager to dissolve itself in it. Mystery of the reconstituted androgyne, long wedding night where the two natures are reconciled by the conjoined virtue of the great secret forces: Sulphur – Mercury – Salt.

"But in this operation, magical above all others, of which mortals only know the simulacrum, nothing can be accomplished without the breath of the Sublime Father.

"So it is that each being is a carrier, from its beginning – like a sealed letter – of the spark of eternal fire; that gives, with the supernatural power of transmission, that which animates matter, recommencing on its own account the act of the creator. This, my son, is the supreme secret. But the secret of secrets is that men, reduced for the most part to a functional life, totter and tremble to the vertiginous poles of the translation of life, *without even knowing what they are doing!* Their thickness is such that they find the double magical operation of conception and birth *quite natural!* They desire, they couple, they play in an obscure delirium that makes them like quadrupeds. In the interplay of the flesh they see only the earth. They are blind servers of the silt and future corruption. They do not dream of the soul. In the nuptial spasm they forget to summon Heaven!

"Is it true, as the ancestors affirm, that it was a man, in the beginning, who stole the heavenly fire? Strange adventure in truth, and well made to blind us to the prodigious powers that the Father had allotted to his creature! But it appears certain on the other hand that the Spirit of Evil has taken possession of the World, and that the use of Fire – that eminently sacred thing – has been falsified and perverted by the children of the Earth. The fire of the wise or the fire of love now consumes only souls wandering or already in exile. The conflagration lit by hatred is nowhere near extinguished. And this is the seed of fury that passes on the blood of the culpable.

"Inextinguishable is the flame of envy, the flame of vengeance, the flame of fratricidal strife. The same, Adragante, as that which threw, at the battle of Arderidd, the Saxons against the Bretons, the son against his father. The nourishing fire, the healing fire, the saving fire, man has made an auxiliary to his folly. The Earth provides the metal to serve the needs of destruction, and fire achieves the work of death."

Merlin stopped for a few moments, then raised both hands before him in a gesture of conjuration. He continued in a lower voice:

"O my son, if you saw, like me, the cruel future that the race of men prepares for itself! The conflagrations crackle. The pyres are lit. Great cities burn in the red nights of History. And thousands of living torches consume themselves, howling on the wheel of the zodiacs for long centuries."

Once more the Master fell silent, then his eyes began to sparkle. He prophesied: "But a day will come when the fire will cease to be directed against himself. After nameless cataclysms that will menace even the existence of the globe, the world will renew. It is then that the houses of the Sun will be turned upside down and the twelve signs of the zodiac will give battle on the stellar plains. The Lion against the Bull, the Ram against the Goat, and when the hour strikes when the Envoy of the Sublime Father comes to judge the generation of the Water Bearer, one will see the resuscitated Virgin descend from the Sky on the back of the Centaur. And she will place a bare foot on the head of the Scorpion, and the Sun will give birth to the dawn of Reconciliation. The leopard and the lamb will lie down together in the fields, the bird of prey guard the goldfinch under its wing, and the dragon watch over the sleep of the newly born. Such will be the work of the celestial Fire, by which the Earth will be purified."

Having approached the chimney, Merlin struck a gong. The two gnomes reappeared, carrying strange tools of which I did not know the use. At a sign from Merlin, they leaped on the earthen vase that I had noticed on entering the hall, put it on a sort of tripod and opened it with infinite caution. Then they left as they had come, as light as elves.

"Watch!" Merlin told me, taking me by the arm, showing me the interior of the vat where a molten gleaming and golden material boiled.

"This is the work of the Fire, Adragante. There is the arcana of the Wise. When this matter in ignition solidifies, if I wanted I could make enough gold ingots to raise a fleet or buy an army of mercenaries. But be reassured, this treasure will be reserved for other things."

The surprise petrified me. Merlin took a long golden spatula and began to stir the liquid.

"I will teach you later," he continued, "the process of the Great Work, of which only a few initiates have been given the secret."

He showed me the sheets of lead. "It is with this," he said, "that I obtain that."

And in the spatula he held out to me I saw – actually saw – a few drops of gold in the mixture.

"It is thirteen moons today, my son, that this fire has burned night and day under the athenor. Thirteen moons! Four seasonal digestions, during which the alchemical trinity is passed through all the stages. Calcination, at first, dissolution, then corruption. It is necessary that the seed die in the darkness of the silo. That is the stage of apparent death, the ever anxious stage of mottled putrefaction. Then comes the lightening announcing the resurgence. Then, progressively the material takes on all the colours of the solar spectrum. Violet, indigo… the weeks pass… green yellow, orange… finally here is the red, the moment of espousal of the Sulphur and the Mercury, of the Sun-King and the Moon-Queen. This is the time when the Mother Goddess allows the birth of the philosophical stone. It only remains for the initiate to project this stone on the metal by fusion in Saturn. I have myself practised the projection in the last quarter of the thirteenth moon, and here, my son, here, the work of sublimation is complete."

While Merlin spoke, the gold began to harden in the bowl. Merlin called the two strange servants again, to whom he gave rapid instructions; then, without another word, he left the room, signing for me to follow him.

IX

Hardly had we left that which I since learnt to be an alchemical laboratory when we found ourselves in a circular room, much darker, where mirrors of different dimensions were hung.

"We are here," Merlin told me, "in the circle of the past, present and future. For it is necessary that you know, Adragante, that ideas of space and time are crutches for our mortal intelligence, and that the unfolding of our life is only a long mirage, of which we only understand the meaning at the moment of our death, which is merged, in a unique light, with that of our birth. That will be as if we had never been. Try to understand that. The drop of sperm from which you have come, and which is nothing itself but a spark of matter, will be the exact equivalent of your corpse, that will return into the unthinkable to develop new seed. But your soul – the only truly living thing, and consequently eternal, since it has no beginning nor end – will provisionally be reclothed with a phantom that you will have constructed in the astral light. Your appearance, always perceptible in the prodigious stores of memory, will be the result of a part of your destiny, and the other a part of your active will in the fullness of free will. Later, machines themselves will have memory, and will be able to give at any moment the *illusion* of your 'presence', to show you living to your friends, even though you had long returned to dust."

Merlin showed me the mirrors attached to the wall. "But from now our mirrors remember. What am I saying? That they are superior over future machines *in that they remember the FUTURE!* It is thus, my son, that I can show you, in one of them, your early childhood. But I can equally show you other things."

Here the Master stopped and looked at me for some minutes in silence:

"You are not yet an adept, but I have not forgotten that you have been resuscitated, that is to say twice-born, and that I have chosen you to be my disciple. Arm yourself with courage, Adragante, and look!"

The Master seized my arm firmly and led me toward a great obsidian mirror, slightly convex, which was fitted into the stone. Then he took two dried branches – one of mistletoe and the other of vervain – and lit them at one of the lamps.

A thick smoke rose before the mirror, while Merlin explained that vervain, culled according to rites taught by magic, is a plant that gives second sight.

When the smoke cleared, I saw all at once in the dark mirror a plain as far as the eye could see that I soon recognised as that of Salisbury. And what was my stupor when I saw the phases of that terrible battle unfold before me, that had cost the life of King Arthur and the Knights of the Round Table! But as all this passed in silence, although I still had within my ears the frightful noise of the mêlée, I persuaded myself that I was the butt of a nightmare. Suddenly my heart froze when I saw myself, mortally wounded by a Saxon javelin and trampled under the feet of the horses. I felt at that moment the same physical pain that had brought me down on the field of battle, and almost fainted…

"Look again," he told me.

When I reopened my eyes, the scene had changed. The plain was, so to speak, deserted, but fuming and strewn with many bodies. I was dead; Merlin carried me in his arms. Then the mirror having become completely dark, I thought the vision ended, and turned toward the Master, who remained impassive.

The mirror opened again, and I saw an immense lake surrounded by fir trees that seemed to rise to the sky. In the middle of this lake a hand rose and brandished a sword, and at the same moment all the approaches to the lake were peopled with shadows that glided rapidly on the bank, and among whom I recognised with fright all my massacred companions – Bliais du Chatel, Morzol, Iwerzon, Remendall, Krouadur, Pesked, Ker-Noaz, Driant de la Forest, Maret de la Roche, Bohor de Carhaix, the Seneschal… And one after the other they came to the centre of the mirror, that they filled bit by bit with their mortal silhouettes. Their closed eyes opened on glassy pupils, their lips moved as if they wanted to offer some words, then they vanished like clouds. Arthur finally appeared, wearing his crown, his handsome face framed by white hair, dressed in armour, his hands crossed on the hilt of his sword. It was just as I had seen him on the field of battle. He opened his living eyes and looked at me, at which I could hardly stand. Then at a stroke the vision faded.

"The spectres you have seen," said Merlin, "have nothing in common with their souls. Later I will explain the ways of the second death, and that which defines the earthly part and the eternal part in all creatures."

There was then a long silence during which Merlin lowered his eyes to the ground. A light fluttering agitated his eyelids and I had the impression that he hesitated, or at least that he awaited an inspiration to act…

"Come," he said brusquely, "it is important that you see this too."

Merlin began his incantation before another mirror, and I then saw a river in a verdant country where many apple trees and flowers grew. Then a red-headed man appeared, dressed in garments of goat skin, and followed a flock that descended the hills. They were suddenly assembled at a sort of ford where the river appeared almost dry. A man appeared, whom I could not at first recognise, but on seeing him more clearly was struck with insurmountable anguish. He was tall and wore the white robe of the druids. The shepherds shook their fists at him, then one of them picked up a stone from the stream and threw it in his direction. The man put his hand to his throat and showed them a shining star. Scarcely had I recognised Merlin, my beloved Master, when a hail of stones struck him. He fell… and I saw his bloodied face, his forehead broken by a frightful wound. He again made a gesture, as if to defend himself. The crowd threw themselves on him in a confused mêlée and what I saw then was so truly horrible that I ended by uttering from my dumb throat the cry of a wounded beast, and I fell unconscious before the mirror.

X

When I awoke I found myself lying on a camp bed, in quite a spacious room, surrounded by heavy curtains. It was bathed in red light of which I could not find the source, for the room did not have any lighting. A heavy smoke arose from an incense burner spreading a strong odour of benzoin and myrrh. I was alone. On sitting up on my couch and leaning on one of the cushions that surrounded me, I saw they had undressed me, and clad me in a robe of red silk, under which I was completely naked. How long had I slept? I had no way of knowing, not even if it was day or night. What was this mysterious room? And what had become of the Master?

I rubbed my eyes and looked about me. Then I saw behind the incense burner a strange seated statue that made me shudder. It was an idol in the form of a goat that had the attributes of both sexes. It had a beard, and from its forehead, where the same star shone as that of Merlin, came two immense curved horns. Two great black wings were deployed behind its naked body, which was that of a woman. A robe enveloped its legs and thighs up to the height of its diaphragm. Between its thighs, representing the male sex, rose a caduceus on the scaly wheel of a zodiac. The right hand joined the index and middle finger in an initiatory gesture, raised to the sky; the left hand pointed to the earth. Under the robe, its two legs crossed on a sphere ending in the hooves of a goat.

I had hardly returned to my senses when the hangings that faced my bed slowly opened to reveal an alcove in which spread a more rosy light. I was only separated from this alcove by a transparent veil and my heart began to beat wildly when I saw a naked young woman on a satin couch smiling at me. Her red hair surrounded her down to the small of her back and her two white arms, folded behind her head, revealed the mother of pearl creases of her armpits. A rush of blood rose in my virgin body and I found myself before the alcove, from which the netting fell to give me passage, while the adorable creature sat up on her bed and offered me her open arms, her lips moist and crimson.

I was about to succumb in this unexpected invitation when I remembered in a flash the teachings of the Master. I was at a crossroads faced with one of those decisive moments, without any apparent solemnity, on which almost always the direction of one's destiny depends. What pushed me towards this unknown woman if not the instinct of possession that slept in the loins, the purely animal desire, neither striven for nor sanctified by the sacred sentiment of love? For the delight of a few seconds, could I, the risen from the dead, run the risk of renouncing the steps of initiation begun by Merlin? But I could not forget the marvellous embrace of the Bard and Viviane, and I felt the sadness of leaving the world for ever without having felt at least once the ecstasy of sex in my flesh.

At that moment the young woman rose, and clasping her body to mine, put her arms round my neck and sought my mouth. I felt her breath of crushed vervain and with a supreme effort turned my head to escape this dizziness. It was then my eyes met those of the goat faced idol darting at me and shining like two devouring flames.

The truth came to me. I saw again the scene in the magic mirror of the bloodied face of Merlin. Brutally I tore myself from this collar of living flesh. Surprised, the seductress came back towards me but I repulsed her with barbarous violence, and could do no more than utter a cry, a cry of the dumb, that shook me from head to foot. "Help me, Merlin!"

Suddenly the light went out. In the darkness I heard the beating of my heart. Then from afar I heard the harmony of beautiful music. I was overwhelmed by dizziness and felt for my bed. Hardly had I found it than I dropped exhausted and fell into a deep sleep.

XI

I don't know how long I slept. It was Merlin himself who awoke me. He wore his ceremonial robe, his leather sandals encrusted with gems, and over his long hair the starry crown of the Magi. His harp hung from his shoulder.

He embraced me gently, saying nothing, a thing he had never done until now. Then he clapped his hands and the two gnomes appeared, carrying an aiguière and a basin full of perfumed water in which I could refresh my body and face.

I had eaten nothing for a long time. The Master asked me if I was hungry. As I nodded he gave orders to his two little servants and we ate grilled fish and fruit.

Merlin had me dress in a thick leather tunic and a coat of mail, and said, "Adragante, the time has come to bring your testing to an end. You have already triumphed over the flesh. Today you must conquer fear, and die definitively to yourself. Then you will be an adept. You will become my son, and I can give you the safe conduct – 'Pass, you are pure!'– that the Master gives to his disciples on opening the triple door of the Holy Mysteries."

Having lit a torch, the bard put it in my hand, pushed me into a dark corridor and told me to walk before him. It had been some time since I had seen daylight, or the sun, and I thought this also must form part of the tests that were imposed on me.

The corridor was cut in the rock and sloping, and I slipped on the pebbles. Was Merlin following me? I did not know, but carried on, conforming strictly to his instructions.

Suddenly a terrible wind struck me in the face and blew the flame of the torch towards me. I saw I had come out into a vast gallery, where the wind blew with the violence of a hurricane. In the semi-darkness I had to brace myself with all my strength to shelter the flame that guided me, and not be burnt by it. Now, looking at my feet, I realised with a growing fear that the way on which I trod was narrowing, until it formed a ridge of only 6 to 8 inches, and that it overhung a bottomless abyss. The wind, moreover, raged with redoubled force, and I feared to find my torch go out at any moment.

But I had faith in Merlin. His thought sustained me, as also his presence, which I still felt behind me, despite the silence he had observed since our departure.

My heart constricted, but renewing the challenge, I continued to walk step by step into the shadows, until my foot ceased to find solid ground. The path I had been following stopped over the void, and I could see nothing around me but a dark gulf in whence the storm howled and growled. What could I do?

"Go on!" came the voice of Merlin from behind me.

Go on into this abyss? Did I have to die then? With a horrible vertigo the sweat broke out on my forehead, behind which surged the instinct of self preservation. I stepped back a pace, hesitating at the edge of the abyss.

"Go on, I say," the voice of Merlin commanded once more.

I shut my eyes and launched myself into the void. My torch went out. It seemed that my fall was endless. Then I fell into a thick bed of moss, where I sprawled without being able to get up, for my nervous resistance was at an end.

The contact of the hand of Merlin that I felt rest on my neck helped me regain my senses.

"My child," he said, "here you are in the beyond. You have nothing more to fear. God and Heaven are with you."

Then the mage took me by the arm to lift me up, and we found ourselves before an opening in the form of an arch. Here a beam of light filtered through an indentation in the vault that I recognised as a ray of sunlight.

XII

We went out of this door and found ourselves in a new cavern, much vaster than the others, and lit from place to place with luminous rays in which a diffuse dust sparkled. At the centre arose a colossal tree, at the summit of which three solar rays converged. And under the crevices of the perimeter was accumulated a chaos of rocks covered with green lichen. And springing out from them enormous stems of broom starred with fleshy berries the colour of blood, in a mass of inextricable brambles. Near the tree, which appeared very old, and from which powerful convulsed roots appeared here and there, I remarked on the moss covered ground, colonies of giant pale milk-caps and poisonous boletus whose scarlet crowns were the width of a parasol.

Curiously, the trunk of the tree seemed covered with scales and threw off a phosphorescent light; while the higher branches moved and the roots changed place and shape.

Without saying a word, Merlin took me by the arm and helped me climb near to him on a rock in the form of a prow, several feet above the ground. He collected himself for a moment, then taking up his cithara, began to sing in a low and distant voice.

It was an incantation, a haunting melody, an obsessive call come from the depths of the ages:

You who creep under the pale moon
You who hiss in the sleeping night
Brother of clay unjustly cursed
Supreme intelligence, image of the infinite.

Of the age of gold have memory
Renew the pact and the alliance
You who shed your skin under the waning moon
You who hold the secret of the Sages under your tongue
Was it not to you the Infinite offered unreservedly
The evolution of each to be finished.

Of the age of gold have memory
Renew the pact and the alliance.

While Merlin sang, I heard in the interior of the cavern a strange murmur, and a far whistling as if many herdsmen were calling in their flocks from the rain. The roots moved, the crevices in the rock became lit up, and living. And what I had taken for branches and roots of the tree began to *creep* over the ground in our direction. Horror! We were surrounded by innumerable reptiles of all sizes, some as small as the eels that live in the sand of the shore, and that I had sometimes roasted on the embers… but the others!… ah! the others! My temples were gripped as if in an iron gauntlet and a cold sweat ran down my back when I saw snakes ten or twelve feet long, whose bodies were the size of my legs, extended from one end of the grotto to the other, and advancing on us in an irresistible marine movement. Monstrous undulations which I watched in nameless terror. But I dare not approach the bard, who continued to sing, accompanied by his cithara, as if he saw nothing. But when two or three of the most hideous reptiles at the foot of our rock, with their lidless eyes, arose on their coils and darted their forked tongues at us, I huddled up close to the Master despite myself with a supplicant gaze. Without responding to me, Merlin sang with a louder voice, and I saw that the ophideans, that had reassembled one behind the other, had ceased to advance, and appeared to be listening to the mysterious song of the Mage.

Serpent, you who know the secrets of the Earth
And that Heaven provides with a salutary venom
O three times holy serpent, brother of pure souls
Save your bites for the Wise

Of the age of gold have memory
Renew the pact and the alliance.

Then I saw them all. And the fear left my heart to give place to a marvelling. They seemed to understand the words of the Master, subdued by the chords of the lyre.

Merlin stopped suddenly. And again I was seized by terrible anxiety. The Master had his eyes fixed on the tree, whose trunk had begun to shine like a corselet of precious stones. I then heard a rhythmical noise, a bizarre note, that seemed like the far shock of a hammer on a bronze plate. And I had the impression that the whole tree was turning on itself, unrolling its bark.

The metallic strikes came faster, and what I had taken for the trunk suddenly unfolded with a sinister hissing. The head appeared in a luminous ray, a gigantic head that I recognised to be that of a reptile of colossal dimensions. Terror froze my veins, petrified my body. I recognised the serpent who had wandered in the garden, during the night of love of Merlin and Viviane. And my fright knew no bounds when I saw the monster agitating his greenish head in a sound of bells, and cross with a few undulations the distance that separated it from our platform. At the same moment, a vibration followed by a murmur made me think of a rising wind that precedes a storm. It spread through the ophidian people. Their heads came and went like the tamarisk branches under a wind from the ocean.

Hardly a few feet below us the monster looked at Merlin, balancing its head and neck with the same hallucinating sound that produced a soporific effect on my nerves. It opened its steaming mouth where, the colour of clotted blood, there trembled an enormous bifurcated tongue like a sting.

However, Merlin did not budge. His shining gaze never left the serpent.

This impassiveness restored my confidence, even though all my physical resistance had abandoned me. I remarked the fact that since the stop of the musical incantation the attitude of the reptiles had become more menacing. They were all grouped around their chief, which in a prodigious thrust, reared up its body to the height of Merlin.

I could not take my eyes from this horrible vision. I almost felt upon me the enflamed breath of this rattlesnake with golden eyes, whose dilated mouth – into which my head could easily have passed – showed its poisonous fangs. The scales of its back, striated with large black and yellow patches, bristled like the crest of a weaver fish, and I finally realised that the metallic noise which had so frightened me came from the agitation of its sonorous scales fixed as a train on the reptile's tail.

Then the Master, taking his cithara, sounded an arpeggio of aerial sweetness, that glided like a wave over this living mass of beasts in fury and immobilised them, with the exception of the monster who, by successive swaying, progressively approached its sting toward Merlin's face…

Then came the prodigies: "Gorsiff, king of the serpents, I command you," said Merlin in a loud voice that echoed through the grotto.

The serpent stopped as if subdued and there was no more than a soft jingle from its sinister shock of scales.

Merlin placed his hand on the flat head:

"Ossi… Ossoa!… Ossia…!" the Enchanter articulated slowly.

The serpent was agitated by a long shivering. Then it closed its mouth and fell to the ground like a wet cloth. All the other reptiles did the same.

"Adragante," said the Master, taking me by the hand, "have no fear, and follow me."

I descended the rock with him. We passed through the immobile reptiles. Some moments later we were outside the grotto, at the entrance of a narrow passage that opened to the sea.

XIII

A resplendent sun inundated the bay as far as the horizon, and my heart dilated joyously at the immense murmur of the sea.

We were in a pine wood in the form of a rotunda, our feet walking on the springy ground of fallen needles, breathing the aromatic fragrance of the maritime trees who knew how to conserve their vegetable set during the worst storms. Between their light trunks, the infinite sea sparkled like a molten gulf, starred with myriad solar diamonds. At the centre of the rotunda stood a menhir, the height of a man, at the top of which was carved the mysterious sign of the Triad.

"Your testing is over," Merlin told me. "You have seen the cavern of Cézembre, where the most intelligent animals are assembled and the most repulsive of creation. Thus Providence decided that this intelligence of nature be kept at a distance from ignorant and perverse man, and allow only a few initiates to communicate with these strange creatures. None of them need cause you to fear. None of them."

Here Merlin stopped for a second.

"With the exception of one, who is the king of the reptiles, and who only obeys my orders. The incantatory word I pronounced before you – 'Ossi, ossoa, ossia' – is the language of the serpent, and is only valid in my mouth by virtue of a mysterious power given me by the Invisible ones, who secretly connect me to this redoubtable animal.

"I pray you then, my child, never to forget that. You can command all the serpents of the cavern except for Gorsiff, precious guardian of the sacred tree, who is at the same time a king and a genie, and whose bite, frighteningly poisonous, is absolutely without remedy. No one in the world, not even I, Adragante, can ever restore to life anyone who has known the mortal kiss of Gorsiff, who commands the empire of serpents. The rattlesnake who knows all and can easily penetrate your most secret thoughts, and represents in that cavern, forbidden to humans, the fatality of judgement, justice without mercy, and he is the purveyor of the most implacable of the god of Death…"

And as the Master saw me blanch, he added: "To be on one's guard is one thing, to be afraid is another. Nothing is more evil than fear. If you ever meet Gorsiff, avoid being afraid. Above all avoid hatred, for he would not fail to punish you. Besides, in so far as I am of this world, what fear could you have, since you *know*, as he *knows* himself, that I hold you under my protection? It is necessary despite and against everything, to have confidence with Gorsiff!"

At this moment the sun, passing across the top of the trees struck the top of the menhir, illuminating the sign of the Triad, formed by a perpendicular line between two oblique ones.

"My son," said Merlin, "now is the sacred hour of midday, for this menhir is also a solar boundary marker. Recollect yourself, and look at the three lines that represent the three times holy name of the Sublime Father.

"At the beginning of the world, when God pronounced his Name, Light and Life flowed from his Word. And Menw the Old, the son of Menwyd, saw the light born, under the aspect of three luminous and sounding rays, because *hearing and vision were then identical*. And according to the Form and the Sound, that were inseparable from Life and the Almighty, he traced on Earth the form of the Voice-Light.

"The central ray is an I, which is the letter of divine generation. The two other rays are the letters O and V that represent fecundation of the cosmos, and Love without end that maintains the equilibrium of the eternal forces.

"The Sign expresses the Thing, the Thing is the virtue of the Sign. The symbol reveals to us by its form the meaning of universal correspondences. The world is ruled by the law of the ternary. And God, whose invisible letter is also the sign of Unity, is the synthesis of terrestrial oppositions, whose life and death, in apparent conflict, finally join to abolish the subdivisions of matter.

"Evil is necessary to the world, or that which we have come to call evil. Nothing down here is obtained without conflict, and on this rests all that resists – it is probably necessary that a Mordred existed to engender an Adragante! That is the great secret of human life, only admissible to sovereign souls. It means blood and tears. It requires meeting suffering and death to be worthy of access to a superior plane. There is no other meaning to the tests that have come to be imposed, and that have, for their end, revoking the former life to lead to a new life.

"Strength for you was to pass through the shadows and to go as far as the confines of the abyss, to merit the reward of the burst of the day on the sea, and the divine sun, which is the visible image for our perishable eyes of the Father of the Infinite Light."

Merlin approached the raised stone, and bowed for a few moments, then put his hands to the height of the sacred inscription.

"I salute you, stone of the Sun," he said, "you who symbolise, after the reign of the sensitive vegetation and the thinking man, the coming of the Will, and the mineral hardness of which the diamond, that burns without leaving any ash, is the last stage. I salute you, maternal stone, fiery stone, more precious stone to my eyes than those that sleep in the earth to foment the cupidity of humans.

"Your secret life is closed to the vulgar, but the Mage knows that you contain the star, and that you can be, when horizontal, the stone of sacrifice, and in the vertical, the hard wearing house of God.

"And since you are a solar stone, and that you contain inside you the same fire that animates that far star, whose effluvia moreover furnish the heat of my arteries, I wed my mortal blood to your two sparkling ones, that all will unite in a single flame to mount in the ether to the glory of the heavenly Father."

Then giving me his harp, he bent to pick up a sharp flint from near the rocks that went down to the sea. Then he gathered up an armful of bright yellow gorse that devoured the rays of the sun, and put them in two piles at the foot of the menhir.

Then, with a rapid gesture, he lifted his robe and bared his left arm up to the point for the bleeding, where he drove in with a single blow the point of the flint. The blood flowed, reddening the stone, but not a muscle of his face moved.

Ever impassive, he took in his left hand, where the blood still ran, a handful of gorse and rubbed the flint several times on the menhir producing a long spark that set fire to the gorse already roasted by the sun.

Merlin took from his left hand a broad flat ring that was clear as crystal, then, taking from the second pile another handful of spiny stalks, he focussed the light of the sun with the help of the ring, and set fire to the gorse. And I saw – oh prodigious sight! – a tiny sun crackle, and then with a sudden leap, embrace the vegetation.

The Enchanter mixed the two piles, and some minutes later, by virtue of the conjugation of fire and stone, an immense brazier flamed before the menhir, associating in the same offering the three Kingdoms of nature, and the most imposing star in the sky to the Creator.

Little by little, the top of the menhir became incandescent, and the transfigured face of the Master reflected that light with such intensity that I was obliged to shut my eyes. When I reopened them, Merlin, his two arms extended, had left the ground. His whole body seemed enveloped in a great cloud, and the palms of his hands reflected the rays of the sun.

During this time, I heard come from the sea an otherworldly music mingled with far feminine voices, muffled bells, and the strings of thousands of harps, that reflected the regular fall of the waves on the shore. And pressed by a daimon that came to substitute for myself, I took the cithara of Viviane and began to improvise in unison with this music of the spheres.

An intoxicating fragrance came from the brazier, where the last gorse was consumed, and I passed onto the strings of the lyre the hymn of delirious joy that I felt mounting in my heart. I was truly in the beyond; no longer belonged to the earth. And at this the Master rose slowly into the air, obscured by the smoke of the brazier, and then lost in the flame.

And when the pyre was extinguished I saw no more than the menhir at the foot of which the last cinders glowed, and the sign of the Triad that shone mysteriously in the sun.

PART THREE

I

I remained for some time not knowing if I would ever see Merlin again. I had returned to the lower house, near the rock crystal manor that was now occupied only by sea birds. Summer was already declining, evident from the darkening leaves of the forest, and when evening came, dark clouds passed rapidly over the marine skies in which windows of light announced the equinoctial storms.

Far from worrying me, the magical disappearance of my Master had left me with a feeling of serenity. Indeed, I felt transformed, fortified by the wisdom I had acquired in the course of my initiations. From now on Merlin appeared to me as more than a hero or a mage, and I thanked heaven to have been judged worthy to witness the assumption of such a superman on the cliffs of Cézembre. I was sure he would be forever near me as a visible or invisible guide.

Ah! How far I was from my orphan childhood, on the ramparts of my native city, and the noisy companions of my youth, who were no more to me now than phantoms! A Father had been given me who had brought me to the light by the divine seed of the word, and the new life he had given me, after the battle of Salisbury. I was now ready to sacrifice, to unite my soul ever more closely with his!

Sometimes I took Viviane's harp and went as far as the menhir of the Triad. The sea murmured, the sun caressed the raised stone with its slanting rays, and there I improvised strange songs that glided on the wind into the immensity. Until then, I had never touched a harp string, but the musical gift had come with that of second sight. The seagulls wheeled above my head, and Karantez, come back to the manor, perched on my shoulder.

Then on the first morning of the full moon of September, I saw the barque of Barynthus sailing in the gulf. Having dropped anchor in the shelter of the promontory, he climbed quickly up to the manor.

Barythus was not talkative by nature and I had to be content with the verbal message with which he had been charged. He gave me Merlin's crystal ring, the one he had used in burning the gorse at our last encounter, and informed me that he had the mission to take me on board the *Keravel* and sail towards the West where the sun set. I tried to make him understand by signs how much I wanted news of the bard but he contented himself by shaking his head while inviting me to prepare for departure. He advised me to take a sheepskin, for we were leaving, he added, on quite a long voyage. And he took leave of me by saying, "We have all the provisions on board. I will wait for you on the shore at midday. With the north-east wind it will be a great trip with the wind behind us, and I count on you to help with the sails."

I had been a sailor on board the *Cornwall* so the sea was my element. I inclined my head in sign of assent, and warmly shook the pilot's hand.

By three o'clock in the afternoon we had rounded the Cape of Fréhal, and at the end of day passed onto the open sea by the isle of Bréhat. Barynthus asked me to take the helm and for the following night we took turns.

In the morning the sky was overcast and the wind became north north-west. We ate buckwheat pancakes with smoked fish, along with a good swig of hydromel from the pilot's flask to keep ourselves warm. Barynthus remained silent, and only spoke to shout, in his guttural voice, brief commands of manoeuvre.

I saw him as one of those beings with an ineluctable atavism to be a wanderer of the seas, who loved the risk and sought an obstacle for the pleasure of overcoming it. He was above average height, with broad shoulders, muscular arms, and calloused hands with square finger ends. Under a kind of wide leather bonnet, his straight hair with red highlights framed a weather beaten face, where under bushy eyebrows washed with spray, his blue eyes were so light as almost to be confused with the whites.

At that moment I realised he was looking at the sky with marked attention and a hint of anxiety on his face.

"Bad… bad…" he repeated a couple of times, shaking his head. The sea had got up suddenly like the ridge of a reef at the going out of the tide. A brutal gust of wind made the sails creak and leaned the boat over to starboard. A great wave, surging like a monster, crashed over us and whipped our faces like a fistful of hailstones in a mass of foam.

"Lower the sail, son!" cried Barynthus pulling down his bonnet and buttoning up his top coat, "We've run into a squall."

I ran to reef the sails and hauled firmly on the ropes. The dance had already begun! The main mast groaned in a menacing fashion. We sailed with care, trying to head into the wind. From long experience

Barynthus knew all the channels but the waves drove us towards the dangerous rocks in the vicinity, for we had arrived in view of the Seven Isles.

Suddenly a blue lightning flash tore the sky – followed almost immediately by a clap of thunder. Bronze coloured clouds descended on us like the lid on a bowl.

"Look out!" shouted the pilot. I just had time to cling to the gunwale as a second column of foam swept across the *Keravel* while the sky burst with another sudden strike overhead. Claps of thunder followed one other without interruption and the lightning flashed on all sides, opening the leaden horizon with sinister cracks. The ocean fumed under the gusts. The *Keravel* mounted the crests of the waves almost vertically, that the storm threw at us like walls of liquid marble.

I don't know how long that storm lasted, in the course of which about twenty times the *Keravel* was almost driven onto the rocks. I only remember that towards the end of the day a lull saved us, allowing us to take refuge in a cove sheltered from the west winds. We could drop anchor and rest from our exhausting struggle against the conspiracy of the elements.

At day break, the wind was still quite violent, but Barynthus, having watched the flight of sea birds, affirmed we could once more take to the open sea. During the night I had called on Merlin, while rubbing the ring in my right hand, and begged him to drive away the storm and to bless the rest of our crossing. I had hoped to see him in my dreams, as before in my hut in Broceliande, but no sign was given me, which forced me to abandon our fragile destiny to the will of the heavenly Father. However, on our departure, I noticed that the winds had returned to the north-east and we progressed with full sail toward a bright interval of very good promise. "Wind behind us," said Barynthus, with a grimace I took for a smile. "You can pay out the sail."

I began to do so when I saw on our beam a wide reef of white water on which the keel of a small boat was impaled. Its mast was broken, but still held onto the hull by the torn sail swinging in the foam at the will of the breaking waves. Near the broken boat, through a gap in the rock, I saw two bodies were sprawled.

I went to warn Barynthus but he had already seen and ordered me to take down the sail and drop anchor. Thanks be to God, the sea progressively calmed and without too much difficulty I could soon take to the dinghy of the *Keravel* and row towards the reef.

I tied the dinghy to the keel of the wreck and waded through the breakers that the lowering sea was beginning to uncover. The first of the shipwrecked mariners lay face down on the rocks with both arms extended. On turning him over I saw he was dead from a deep wound that had caved in his skull. He was of middle age, prematurely bald. A fringe of grey beard framed his bony face, and he was dressed in a long brown robe, with leather sandals to protect his bare feet. As he was already cold I tipped him into the sea.

I then approached the second one, who lay on his side, his head of cropped hair lying on a bunch of kelp. He was very young lad whose sleeping face struck me with its beauty. I felt his fine and pointed hands and found he was still alive. The needles of the rocks had torn his clothes and left him with just a leotard and a long torn linen shirt, while deep cuts had bloodied his knees.

I discovered, with some surprise, that he a wore a thin gold chain round his neck from which hung a little wooden cross, in the centre of which a man's face was carved, contorted in agony.

I tried vainly to bring the youth to his senses, but managed to hoist him onto my shoulders and carry him to the dinghy. It was very hard to do so for I slipped on the rocks of the reef with their viscous heads of seaweed, but finally managed to take him back to the *Keravel* where Barynthus and I laid him down in the steerage on a bed of seaweed.

As he was still unconscious I threw a covering over him and rubbed his temples with a little hydromel. He vaguely opened his eyes, but then fell back, without saying a word.

"Adragante! Come and help with the rigging!" cried the pilot in a thunderous voice. "We've already lost too much way with the storm and saving this unknown. You'll have plenty of time to deal with him, have no fear. There are more long days before us between the sea and the sky. So let's hoist the mainsail and prepare to raise anchor!"

And so we continued our voyage westward. The weather was fine and the *Keravel,* pushed by a good wind, leapt through the waves, opening a long wake of silken foam with its passage.

A little later I went down to the unknown one, with a cloth and a bowl of seawater to bathe his wounds. When I began to clean the wound on his right knee he gave a sharp cry, the tone of which made me shiver over this helpless flesh polished like marble. Having lifted his tunic on a thigh as shapely as a statue I began to rub it with the wet cloth, to try to recall him to life and give him some food.

I had taken off his leotard, and then opening his shirt, baring his chest and shoulders. God in heaven! It was like a lightning strike down my spine. Two beautiful young breasts sprang from the tunic that had fallen down to his hips. The shipwrecked young man was a girl!

At that moment she sat up all of a piece, as if the modesty resting dormant in her, that I had innocently violated, had brought her out of her lethargy. With both hands clenched over her bosom she fixed me for a second, her eyes wide, whose blue was darkened under the shock of intense emotion. At the same time she gave a heart rending cry such as I had never heard before, readjusting her shirt with great nervous gestures to shield herself from my gaze. But she could hardly stand up and collapsed, moaning. I stepped forward to help her.

"Get away, demon!" she cried in the tone of a hunted beast. "Don't touch me!"

I stood before her, helpless, unable to reassure her by explaining all that had come to pass.

"Why am I on this boat?" she demanded, "Who are you? And where is my companion?"

She passed a hand across her forehead.

"Ah yes… I remember now. The storm. The raging sea. The wrecking of our boat."

She looked at me again. Despite my silence, she seemed gradually to realise that I meant her no harm.

"Who are you then? Answer me! Why don't you say something?"

Not knowing what to do, I took one of the blankets and threw it over her shoulders. A light of astonishment passed through her eyes, but I was too moved to sustain the flame of her gaze any longer. I climbed up to the bridge to replace Barynthus at the helm, signing to him to look after our shipwrecked passenger.

I imagined what the surprise of the sailor would be in the presence of this young girl, and lost myself in conjecture on the identity of this mysterious creature who, by the will of God, found herself suddenly involved in our destiny.

II

I have said that Barynthus was no chatterer, but the old Celtic pilot had, on the contrary, one of those direct natures forged by contact with the elements, that enabled him at a stroke to enter into connivance with the most wild creatures and obtain their trust.

After a few hours, the unknown had become more relaxed. After having explained to her how she found herself on board the *Keravel*, Barynthus had told her about me and my infirmity, and she knew now that she had nothing to fear. She also knew that her companion was dead on the reef and that she would, for better or worse, have to share the hazards of a long voyage with us.

The wound to her leg was fortunately not serious, and the sailor made a ligature with a cloth dipped in oil. As she was hardly dressed, Barynthus offered her a surcoat and a pair of his trousers. She refused at first for she did not like the idea of being dressed like a man, but in the end accepted the guise.

In the evening she wanted to mount the bridge, supported on the arm of Barynthus, for her ankle made her suffer. I offered her my sheepskin for a seat, and for the first time she smiled at me. Tears wet my eyelids. She saw them, and offered me her hand. At this contact I felt the mysterious affinity established between two souls. But she had turned her head to Barynthus who, squinting before the slanting rays of the setting sun, had taken up the helm again.

It was the end of one of those beautiful September days when the horizon seems flooded with liquid gold. The serenity of the sky, slightly pale, contrasted with the storm of the evening before, and the gentle rocking of the boat caused us to forget the wickedness of the storm. I was charged with distributing the food. Our passenger ate with good appetite some vegetables, two pancakes on which I had spread a little salt butter, and a few plums. But she refused the smoked fish, and also the apple juice, content to drink fresh water from Barynthus's flask.

"You're not an inquisitive man," she said to the pilot, as he put his knife away and took a last swig of hydromel. "You know nothing of who I am or where I come from."

"I don't ask questions," replied Barynthus, "and don't like it much when they are asked of me."

"You could at least ask my name."

The pilot leaned on the tiller without reply. She turned to me, and with a nod of my head I gave my assent.

"My name is Colombe," she said.

I looked at her. The pilot had given her one of his leather bonnets, and Colombe had the air of a cabin boy. She was rather brown, with a face of extraordinary purity, in which opened great light eyes with large pupils. She seemed of a contemplative nature, even though her rather square chin hinted at an implacable will. A little dark mole marked her cheek, and her mouth described an impeccable arc.

"And he," she suddenly asked the pilot, indicating me, "what is his name?"

"He's called Adragante the Gaël. He fought with Arthur, our king. He's one of the Knights of the Round Table."

"Oh!" she said, in great surprise. "And was he born dumb?"

"I've nothing to say about about that," replied Barynthus with a certain brusqueness.

There was a silence. The *Keravel*, supported by the wind, now passed to the open sea at Enès Level. At least this was the opinion of Barynthus, based upon a view of the cove of Goulven, that we believed we could distinguish, despite falling night, before the shore was lost to view. We turned the hour glass once more and I took the helm while the pilot descended into the steerage to take a little rest.

Colombe expressed the wish to stay with me until my change of watch. The night was magnificent and the first stars began to shine in a cloudless sky. I saw to starboard the seven stars of the Great Bear where the soul of King Arthur resided, and of which the three stars of the Tiller and the square of the Chariot represented, according to Merlin's teaching, the creation of the visible universe by the Invisible Triad.

I showed the constellation to the young girl then, with my fingers, indicated successively to her the two numbers – three and four – and their total, waiting for her reaction with great curiosity.

She reflected for a moment and then said:

"I think I understand. They are three pure spirits who pull the chariot of the world. In our new religion, those three spirits become the holy Trinity, as Augustine teaches, one of the great doctors of the new faith. Do you know this sign?"

She touched her forehead, her chest and each of her shoulders.

I shook my head.

"This," she said, "is how we Christians draw on our body the image of the cross on which our Master died for the salvation of the world."

At these words I recalled a tale Merlin had told me before the battle of Salisbury. About his meeting with a hermit in the Caledonian forest and the story of the ignominious death of a sage of the East who called himself the son of God, and whose doctrine of love had begun to spread across the countries of the North. I realised that Colombe must be a sectary of this new religion.

"Here is something I'd never noticed," said the young girl. "The Trinity gives the number Three, but the sign that represents it materially gives the number Four. That's perhaps an explanation of the Mystery. What do you think, sir knight?"

I was astonished at such knowledge allied to a profound lucidity. It was the first time I had met a young woman with such lively intelligence. And I was not slow to admire this creature, born of the sea, like the faeries in our cosmogonies, and who sheltered in a perfect body a soul that was no less perfect. It was absolutely essential that Colombe should meet Merlin. I wished for that with all my strength. But what was she? Where was she going? I burned to know the secret of this Christian virgin.

"Are you a Breton?" she asked.

She divined rather than saw soon my sign of assent, for night had taken possession of the sea, and the moon had just risen and only feebly lit the bridge of the *Keravel.*

"Then you no doubt belong to the religion of the druids, who were my ancestors too," continued Colombe. "For I am Breton as well. But if, as Barynthus said, you are one of the last knights of the Order of the Round Table, you must be something other than a follower of the religion of the forests. For you must certainly have known Merlin the Enchanter who founded that Order."

I could not restrain a quick start of surprise that Colombe noticed, for she continued: "Yes, I know very well that you've approached that strange person from the other side of the ocean sea, about whom there are so many legends. And who has the reputation of being at the same time a great doctor of Celtica and a weaver of spells. I have never seen him, but they speak of him in the Cornish peninsula, which is my country, and which is partly his – although does a being like him have a country? After the bloody defeat at Salisbury and the death of your king, the most diverse rumours circulated about him. Some claimed he had never existed, others that he had fled after the victory of the Saxons, to take refuge with the druids of Broceliande."

While the young girl spoke the moon rose higher over the horizon and its rays, passing through the rigging, illuminated the face of Colombe with a supernatural brightness. I was quite overcome to hear the name of my beloved Merlin pronounced, and for it to come like this was beyond my desires.

The wind had dropped and the boat progressed only with difficulty across the calm surface of the sea while the gentle voice of Colombe rang out like a crystal.

"But I know very well that Merlin was a real person. It was my master Gaodal who first told me about him, in our monastery in Cornwall where he had become the chief priest and where we neophytes learned the rudiments of the Christian religion. He met Merlin in the solitudes of the forests of Caledonia, where he had lived for some years, and who, at the same time, came down the River Clyde towards the cascades of Corra Linn Fall which he wanted to explore. He returned several times to the grotto where the hermit Gaodal had elected to live, and it's there that Merlin received what we call the 'good news'. It seems he was especially moved when he heard about the marvellous adventures of Joseph of Arimathea. In the end Gaodal was greatly surprised that Merlin had never given him the sign of life, for he was convinced he had been converted to the new faith."

Colombe remained silent for a few moments, then carried on in a louder voice, gazing at me. "So it seems impossible that Merlin has never spoken to you of the Christ, and that he left you and your companions of the Round Table in ignorance of the testament of love that the son of Miriam wrote with his divine blood, before dying on the hill at Jerusalem!"

The sand in the hourglass indicated the end of my watch. It was time to awaken Barynthus and to rest in my turn. But as I was about to leave, Colombe anticipated my move and gestured for me to stay at the helm.

"Why awake Barynthus? I'm sure that you're not tired. The night is so beautiful, and I still have many things to tell you. Stay with me for another turn of the hourglass. Please stay… Adragante."

It was the first time she had called me by my name, and I suddenly had the impression that I had always known her. A former sister perhaps? Or, who knows – the divine lover? But as we were delivered, by our reciprocal vocations, from immediate servitude to the flesh, all physical desire was irrelevant. It was simply our two souls that embraced each other, in harmony and serenity. It was not only the turn of an hourglass that I would have gladly given to Colombe – but the whole night – all my life! However I feared for her fatigue after the events of the past day and showed my anxiety by indicating her knees and the wound to her leg.

"Don't be afraid of that," she said, smiling. "I can forget my body whenever it's necessary. Tomorrow, if I know how to pray to God, my leg will be cured. Nothing is more beautiful, nothing more effective than prayer, and our brother from Calvary is always with us. The holy Gaodal often told me so, and how one day he gave sight to a blind man…

"But now Gaodal is dead," she added, lowering her voice. "It was he who accompanied me in the little boat which was to take us to Brittany. He was the one you found with his head broken, on the reef where we had been thrown by the storm, when we were in sight of the coast. May the Angels receive his pure and beautiful soul and the will of God be done!"

"Even at the heart of the worst sufferings," she reflected, "we must have faith in God, whose plans overwhelm and escape us. I could not have come on board the *Keravel*, I could not have met you – with all the consequences that brought it about – without the shipwreck and the death of Gaodal. The splendour of the Christian religion, you see, Adragante, is to have given a meaning to pain, and to have made its acceptance one of the most beautiful things in the world!"

The more I heard the words of Colombe the more I found their analogies with those of Merlin. They both joined, in different ways, at the same crossroads of light. Ah, how I longed to see them meet, and hear them confront each other and discuss these doctrines! But Barynthus had said nothing, and I did not know where or when I might see the Master again.

"I suppose," continued Colombe, "you must have been quite intrigued when you saw I had sacrificed my hair. It is necessary you know that, despite my Celtic origins, I was brought up by a Christian family, and baptised on the day of my birth by an anchorite who wanted to give me the name of one of my ancestors, who was martyred in the reign of Marcus Aurelius for confessing the faith of Christ. My youth was most studious. I lived in the company of learned doctors who successively initiated me into the doctrines of the new religion. I had reached the marriageable age when I met the monk Gaodal, who had himself been converted to Christianity by a holy traveller come from the shores of the Mediterranean to the country of Cornwall.

"Gaodal was an apostle doubling as a miracle worker. He exercised a very great influence on me, and it was he who made me determined to consecrate myself to the Lord. Having given my vows I cut off my hair as a sign of mortification and obedience, and took the veil. A little while later Gaodal declared I had the qualities required to take the apostolate, and I began my mission with the pagans in the Isle of Britain.

"Then it was decided we should follow the example of the first monks from Ireland, and go and evangelise our brothers in Armorica. Perhaps you know that monasteries have already been founded, and we should soon meet some of our monks, who are established on the south of a peninsula facing the great ocean. Unhappily our craft wasn't strong enough to last such a long journey. You know the rest."

Colombe fell silent, then made the sign of the Christians and put her two open hands together one against the other. She shut her eyes and her expression became as impenetrable as a statue. I heard her recite a kind of incantation in a language unknown to me. Even so, her voice became softer and softer and suddenly her head fell to her chest. Fatigue had finally vanquished her. Colombe was asleep.

I ran to the steerage to awaken Barynthus, who went to take up the direction of the *Keravel*. My heart beat as I leaned over the young girl to lift her and take her in my arms. I feared she would awake. But she remained in total abandonment as she seemed to have come to the end of her strength. She was no more than a poor defenceless creature. She belonged to me completely, and I felt the weight and warmth of her body against me. With infinite care I put her down on the berth, laid her out on the seaweed mattress and covered her with my sheepskin.

She was as lonely as me, separated for ever from her spiritual companion, without any support but the faith that animated her and projected her into an unknown world towards those she called her brothers. In the faint light of the lantern hung in the steerage, I looked on her pure face, delivered to the mysterious powers of sleep. An irresistible urge pushed me towards Colombe, who appeared more and more like a gift from God, and in whom I already saw the 'promise' of eternal nights. I stretched out at her side and gently took her sleeping hand, which offered no resistance. And while the boat glided in silence over the midnight waves, in a cradle like movement that led us to the bounds of innocence, we slept together, hand in hand, like two children lost in the depths of the sea.

III

The next afternoon the *Keravel* easily rounded the point of Kermorvan, before the isle of Béniquet. The wind had mounted to northward and we were conducted easily across this passage at the sill of the door of the Ocean always feared by navigators. Fair weather clouds maintained themselves on the horizon, without ever masking the sun, and Barynthus announced that he hoped to reach the highest point of Armorica before nightfall.

Colombe could now move about the bridge, leaning on my shoulder. She seemed quite happy to share the duties and even asked Barynthus if she could take the tiller to show her nautical capabilities.

"It's two years since I sailed boats round the coasts of Cornwall," she said to the pilot, "but even with these cuts to my legs I could show that I'm not incapable of handling one."

As the sea was still quite calm, Barynthus agreed to trust the helm of the *Keravel* to the girl, and we were surprised at the skill with which she steered us for several miles.

"Make for the cape to the west," ordered the pilot.

"Where are we going?" she asked brusquely. "We've been sailing for hours and hours and you haven't told me the end of your voyage."

"You'll know soon enough," replied Barynthus. "My orders are to reveal nothing before we reach land."

"You're sailing under someone's orders then?"

"May be," responded Barynthus. "Meanwhile, give me back the tiller. We're coming to the difficult bit."

To starboard the sun descended rapidly towards the sea, and its reddening disc seemed to light up the surface of the waves. The swell became longer and curled lightly under the September evening breeze.

"It will soon be night," said Colombe. "The time has come to lift our souls toward the Lord, and ask him to extend his holy protection on our ship."

"Come along Adragante," she told me, taking my fingers, "join your hands like me and link our souls in prayer. You too, Barynthus, who know the dangers of the Ocean. Put your fate and that of the *Keravel* into the hand of He who commands the storms, and without whose permission we can neither suffer nor perish."

Colombe's voice suddenly became serious, and her beautiful forehead, made golden by the last rays of the sun, turned towards the sky.

"Our Father," she began, "you who have sent your Son for the salvation of the World, hear the prayer of your servant Colombe and your server Adragante, met today by your will under the sign of the Cross.

"Since it is through love for us that the Child Christ accepted to die so that all humanity could be reborn, it is in the name of Love that we address your Power, and ask that you watch over the children who have been made from your clay, and who are subject to the same earthly weaknesses.

"Enlighten the blind who live without understanding the meaning of their suffering, and bring them in from the shadows.

"Keep us in the Light you have given us. Ever have for us the tenderness of a Father!

"And you, Christ, who consented to descend for us from the condition of Creator to that of creature, let your spilled blood not be in vain, and let your sacred emanations give to all our brothers, known and unknown, the Resurrection and the Life.

"Protect our friends, our enemies, and the friends of our enemies!

Send the Angel of the Sea to guide our little ship, and make it come without danger to the haven of your desire!

"Finally, O Lord Christ, be willing to receive into your heavens the soul of your server, my holy Master Gaodal, that you have recalled to you by the mysterious ways of the ocean. May your will be done, for it is to you alone and to your Father, through all the centuries, to whom belong the Kingdom, the Power and the Glory."

"So may it be!"

Tears shone in the eyes of Colombe as once more she made on her body the sign of the Christians. As for me, I was overcome by such a radiant force, and put into the height of happiness by the fact that she had wanted to associate my name to hers in this strange invocation where she went so far as to pray for her enemies. A strange foment rose in me. I had the feeling that Colombe had taken possession of my soul.

"Look out!" said Barynthus suddenly. "We are now in the Raz de Sein. Haul in the jib, Adragante, and reef the sails securely."

Since the going down of the sun, darkness had fallen rapidly over a sea that suddenly became more swollen. Frothing waves pushed by contrary currents struck against us from all sides and a threatening wind blew on the *Keravel* in short gusts. Far off, to port, a group of fantastic rocks reared up like an immense wall, from which lines of waves unfurled with a striking whiteness.

"The Pointe du Raz," said Barynthus, pointing a finger at the swirling foam. "A cursed spot where daughters of the sea pull sailors, by their feet, to the bottom. Ahoy Adragante! Get ready to tack! We are heading into the wind."

The *Keravel* began to ship water, and the spray shot all over us. The sails clattered in the wind as we tacked back and forth, but Barynthus had rounded the cape.

"You're going toward the coast," Colombe cried suddenly, pointing a finger towards the land, that we could just see, despite night falling, by a line of foam that whitened the shore.

"Yes Colombe, we're going to land on the Isle of Sein."

"Is that the end of your voyage?"

"You'll see," the pilot replied simply, giving a violent pull to the tiller to avoid a crashing wave.

We were now a little way off the rocky coast, but the growing darkness made manoeuvre very difficult, and the sea, under the force of the wind, continued to grow in intensity, taking a savage aspect again.

We struggled for several hours, struck by torrents of foam, and we could not have retained our safety without the skill of Barynthus, who had a sort of divinatory gift to 'sniff' a rock. Colombe called her Christian god to our rescue and to help us as much as he permitted the use of his force to change the wind and tides.

Finally Barynthus managed to find a channel by which we were able to reach land, when, at a few cable lengths from the coast, Colombe, who had gone up to the fore of the *Keravel*, took a false step and fell into the sea with a great cry.

"Save her, save her!" Barynthus shouted, "and hang on to the anchor rope when I throw it off the port side."

I tore off my clothes with desperate haste and plunged naked into the dark, feeling my way through the waves. I heard no more and alas I could not call out. Never have I felt the infirmity that prevented me from communicating with my fellow men in so cruel a way. But the old pilot, who had dropped the anchor, was already on the prow, crying into the darkness…"Colombe! Colombe!"

"Help me Merlin," were the dumb words that I could not pronounce with my lips.

A weak groan came from my right. It was no doubt the response of the Master! Colombe was found! Colombe was in my arms… held tight to my body! And I thanked heaven for granting me such a mystical espousal.

But Barynthus, leaning over the bow of the *Keravel*, could see nothing and know nothing. Despite my joy, I felt my strength declining. With a supreme effort I reached the anchor cable and pulled it with all the strength I had left to make the ship respond. Barynthus understood and came to the rescue. He threw me a rope, which I was able to grasp, while he seized Colombe in his powerful hands.

Then it was my turn. But when the old pilot had hoisted me onto the bridge near the still inert body of Colombe, I felt I had passed the limit of my resistance, and that I was close to death. I could feel no more than a whirl of thoughts and feelings as I passed out.

IV

To lose consciousness is to be cut off from the world. Better and more deeply than in sleep, notions of time and space are distorted or abolished. A century is an hour. An hour a century. When I came back to myself I had the sensation of emerging from a very long sleep.

Someone held my hand. I slowly opened my eyes, and what should be my joy when I recognised Colombe sitting at the head of the bed on which I lay.

"Drink," she said, offering me a cup. "Don't try to hold it. You're still too weak."

I had a fierce thirst. While Colombe supported me on the pillow and helped me drink I looked at her surreptitiously.

In my inability to ask questions about my condition and the length of my illness, I made an effort to raise my hand to try to make myself understood, but my weakness was such that I fell back on my couch without being able to make the least movement.

"Have faith in God," Colombe told me. "It was he who permitted you to save me from the waves, and it is also to him that you owe your own life."

"Which god? Yours or mine?" said a voice that made me shiver.

The door of the room opened. Merlin, my beloved Master, was there before me!

"The god of the Christians, the God of Calvary," replied Colombe to Merlin, while the latter approached my bed and grasped my hand with paternal solicitude.

"Happy to see you again, my son. You have been very ill. Later I will tell you all that happened."

He placed his two hands on my burning forehead, and then turned to the young girl.

"Colombe," he said, familiarly, as if he had known her for a long time, "there is only one god, who is unknowable and unthinkable, and who has no known form for our mortal eyes. The one of whom you speak is only one of the sons of God, since he was materialised in a body and died on the cross, like a man."

"He is the Only Son of God."

"What proof have you of that?"

"His life and his miracles, his death and resurrection."

"There are other sons of God capable of the same spells."

"Perhaps. But no one until him had brought a message like his own. Is it to you, who knew Gaodal in the forests of Caledonia, to whom I must recall the lesson of love that Christ gave to men by sacrificing himself voluntarily on the cross to deliver us from sin, and breaking forever the gates of death?"

"I recognise the importance of his mission, which seems to me marked with the signs of the divine. But the ancient Wisdom teaches us that it is only by successive transmigrations, and not with a single ascent, that man, come from the Abyss and fallen into the circle of Abred, can traverse all forms of existence before meriting the complete love of god and the luminous Sphere of Gwynfyd."

"A creature of god has only one life."

"What permits you to affirm like that what you can only know by hearsay? Have you the pretention, at 20 years of age, to know more than the Magi, the guardians of the arcana of the world, who spent their days and nights in search of the Great Secret? Do you even know who you are? From whence you came? Where you are going?"

"I came from God and I shall return to Him, after the test of the earth."

"Has nothing ever happened to remind you of having been… something else?"

"What are you trying to say?"

"I mean reminiscences that sometimes come to us, in brief enlightenments, the witness of former lives. Have you had no impression, at certain moments, of recovering more than you know? In the light of ancient days, I see you very well, Colombe, a sea swallow on the dunes, or a hind bounding in the clearings of Broceliande."

"Those are the words of a magician. I am not a faery, Merlin, but a creature of God, sanctified by the rite of baptism."

The Master shivered for a second, then continued with a certain vivacity.

"But the religion that you and others like you seek to substitute for that of our ancestors, is that absolutely pure of magic? What are the miracles you talk about? In whose name did this son of god cure the sick and revive the dead?"

"In the name of the living God of whom he is the earthly representation. The power of magic, born of pride, is delegated by the evil Angels."

"Don't you think it could be an act of pride on your part to claim to your own profit the power of miracles, and to hold all that does not bear the seal of your god to be magic or sorcery?"

"It is for God to make the difference, for he alone knows the secrets of our heart."

"Do you believe, young lady, that we all live, myself and my Masters, in error and shadows? That before the coming of your new god, our inspirations, beliefs and powers were delegated to us by evil Angels?"

"I believe so."

"Will you go so far as to declare that the Sublime Father, of whom all my life I was the obedient servant, and for whom generations of druids and the faithful have imposed on themselves a life of renunciation and spiritual perfection, is also only an emanation of the shadows?"

"I hold him to be a false god."

"Then you know the difference between the unnamed Father, who was the light of Celtica, and the God of Israel of whom your Jesus of Nazareth called himself the only son?"

"Yes."

"But why should not this Jesus, in some way, be the son of our Father as well?"

"There is only one God, there cannot be several."

"One can invoke the same god under different names."

"You have already said just now that your god has no name."

"The god of Israel has 77 of them, according to the Kabbalah."

"The number matters little, he is always the same."

"How do you know?"

"It is part of our dogma."

"Was there then a dogma in the teaching of Christ?"

Colombe hesitated a second.

"Yes," she said, "the institution of the Holy Sacrifice."

"A rite at most," interrupted Merlin, "not a religion. It is your doctors, that is to say *men*, who have founded the Christian religion."

"The men who received the tongues of fire, the men visited by the Holy Spirit."

"And whose successors reject us as pagans, under the pretext that they are the only ones to hold the eternal truths."

"Truth imposes itself like the Light. The apostle St John said so."

"Admit however that this Truth, that comes to us from the East, does not give us all the same evidence. What proofs do you bring to convince us?"

"Our innumerable martyrs."

"We also have voluntary victims with the Druids. If I have come to the Isle of Sein, and the convent of Morgane, it is to try to put an end to those abominable practices."

"Our martyrs have proclaimed their faith in the midst of most terrible tortures. Our apostles cured the sick and raised the dead. Believe me, Merlin, the true God is with us!"

"I don't believe, Colombe, in that kind of proof. But since you put me to the challenge, by accusing me of practising with evil forces, I can undeceive you if you like."

The Master extended his arm toward my bed.

"Adragante, who is lying in this room is still, as you know, in a state of great weakness. The admirable devotion you have shown to him during those nights when you fought with death, when you did not realise my presence, is sufficient witness of the affection you have for him. Now, you mutually owe each other your life. You are, I could say, two children, one of each other."

At this revelation brought to me about the young girl, tears filled my eyes.

Merlin continued. "So I have no need to ask if you would be happy to see Adragante completely cured."

Colombe bent her head without reply.

"Well, since your Christian god gives to those who believe in him the power to perform miracles, perhaps you could do something for Adragante. Perhaps you can cure him?"

"A test is necessary for human perfection, and it is by acceptance of suffering that we merit our health. Do you believe that our god holds human suffering in vain? Do you imagine that he has come down among us to make a bed of roses of our earthly existence? To abolish the misfortunes that we need to purify and enoble us? It is in respect for our freedom that God does not always obey the supplications of his creatures."

"If you resign yourself so easily to the bad, why do you seek to convert those you call pagans by miracles?"

"I ask god, in the measure that his mighty Power could grant my prayers, that if he accords me a miracle, it is because that miracle was necessary to show his Glory."

"Then why not try to show that glory to my eyes, by curing Adragante here and now?"

Colombe went pale, and I saw she was biting her lips so as not to respond.

"Is it lack of confidence in your god," continued Merlin, "that you do not ask an immediate cure for the one who saved your life?"

Colombe hesitated to answer… and that hesitation overcame me, for I realised that we had touched the greatest secret of her soul.

She looked at me, as if, in that solemn moment where two superior souls confronted each other, my presence could hamper her response. Then she said, almost in a whisper, lowering her eyes, "It is not for lack of confidence in my god, but through lack of confidence in the… purity of my prayer. And I dare not invoke heaven in that circumstance."

"Explain yourself freely," said Merlin. "No one here is afraid of the truth."

"Well," responded Colombe, "I believe that our god does not permit us to accomplish miracles unless it is a question of impersonal things. The less our prayer is disinterested, the more chance we have to see it granted."

"I see," said Merlin. "For you to ask for the cure of Adragante is to risk a refusal, and to reveal a feeling about yourself."

"For pity's sake stop," cried Colombe going towards the door.

"Why are you so frightened?" said Merlin, barring her way. "Does your god forbid you to love what he has created in his own image? To divert your love for him onto one of his creatures?"

At these words I made a great effort to rise from my bed and beg Merlin to stop a conversation that would be irreparable between Colombe and me. That he shut up and open the door for the girl.

"Where are you going?" he asked Colombe.

"To find my brothers and take them the message from Gaodal."

"But doesn't Adragante still have need of you and your care?"

In the doorway, Colombe regarded Merlin with strange fixity.

"My presence here is useless from now on, for I *know* that you are going to cure him."

"I could not cure him completely, as you know," said the Mage, staring at her in his turn.

"I would not betray his confidence!" Colombe responded fiercely, turning her head towards me, and looking at me with an infinite gentleness. "As for the rest, it is up to the grace of God!"

"But this grace you speak of. Do we merit it, or does God give it to us anyway? Can you communicate it to your fellow men?"

"Yes, by love."

"What love?"

"That which Christ taught us at the Last Supper, and which travels with the mysterious chalice."

There was a pause, during which I could hear my heart beating in my breast. Despite my veneration for Merlin, I secretly wished for the victory of Colombe. Never had I heard such words fall from the mouth of a young girl. Was there then in this new religion something, a certain virtue, that could accomplish a miracle surpassing all others?

"You have the soul of a Knight of the Round Table," Merlin said finally.

"I thank you for your witness," responded the young virgin. "And I thank you above all for having put me to the test. For I firmly believe that you are one of us, despite certain appearances."

"Colombe," said Merlin, "will you give me your hand?"

"Let me embrace you Master. Are you not the greatest of all?"

She did as she had said, then crying "Farewell", disappeared with the lightness of a fawn.

Merlin looked at me for a long time in silence.

V

As Colombe had predicted before she left, I was cured by Merlin, and the same day I could quit my bed and travel over the Isle of Séna. The sky was covered with great heavy clouds, and on this isle of such small dimensions, surrounded by menacing waves, and beaten by the winds of the ocean, I had the impression of being on the bridge of a ship.

The thought of Colombe did not leave me, since I had acquired the certainty that we both loved each other. I was also very worried, and asked myself how she could leave the island in the middle of that storm and regain the coast of Armorica. That is why, by travelling across these deserted and wild lands, my sole occupation was to find the cove where we must have disembarked from the *Keravel* and to see Colombe again if possible before her departure.

I found myself in a ravine, bordered by thick bushes and withered ferns, the stems stiffened by autumn, when I saw Merlin coming to meet me. His face, usually calm, seemed worried. He carried an oar on his shoulder.

"I've come from the little port," he told me. "It's there you were no doubt going, to try to see Colombe again. Listen, I've learned from Barynthus, who stayed on board the *Keravel,* that he hasn't seen the girl. None of the three sea-going boats near Morgane's vessel having left the creek it is impossible for Colombe to have been able to cross the channel, which is very dangerous today. Merlin looked at me with a solicitude that caused my heart to flutter.

"What can have become of her," he continued, "in this island, beyond the manor where Colombe watched over you for three days? There is only the convent of the nine Sènes and the residence of Morgane, King Arthur's sister. She who once wanted me for her lover, but hates me today because I have undertaken to tear the sacrificial knife from the hands of the druidesses. I had come to make a pact with her, to try to convince her to put an end to these cruel rites, in order to save the religion of the ancestors. But Morgane, ever jealous, and come to terms with Skléra, has joined her College of druidesses. After a particularly bloody ceremony to defy me, she forbad my entrance to the convent, with atrocious imprecations and threats of death. 'May he come to find his tomb here. He will never leave Séna alive!'"

Merlin took my arm and we turned back towards the manor. A fine rain began to fall with the night and the west wind whipped rudely in our faces.

"There exists a fatality," continued the Mage whose each word I followed with growing anxiety, "a mysterious chain of events against which the highest and most pure will ends by confessing its powerlessness. No one then can do anything, Adragante, no one, not even the Sublime Father. None can intervene to counteract the initial and eternal rhythm of the universe. No action, no miracle, can go beyond the impassable circle of the laws of the universe. If I throw a stone into space, it will fall back precisely at a given and intended point. All the misfortunes of the world come from a rupture of equilibrium provoked by the liberty of man, and we have no other solution, before the immanence of a misfortune, than to find a new point of equilibrium."

I listened to Merlin, but, I confess, could not drag my thoughts away from the inexplicable disappearance of Colombe. The Master divined this, for he went on: "I have no doubt that we shall end up by finding Colombe, but it would have been better she had never set foot on this Ocean island, which is the absolute fief of Morgane, and where I only awaited you and Barynthus to take to the sea again. The wreck that obliged you to take Colombe on board, her accident and your illness that delayed our departure, finally the too long prolongation in this place of a Christian virgin, are unforeseen events that have upset all my plans and created a new situation, of which I cannot foresee the consequences. We are once more in the hands of fate."

We had advanced across the gorse whose sharp points scratched my legs. Far off, in the twilight, where the murmur of the sea was amplified, we saw sinister lights that moved rapidly like the flames of a pyre. Piercing cries of women, strange vociferations, came as far as us, carried by the wind, and cut me suddenly to the heart.

"You see over there," Merlin told me, seizing my arm, "the den of the priestess Morgane, and that damned soul Skléra. When I think that in these same confines a short time ago the guardians of the sacred fire lived, the nine druidesses of the Isle of Séna, from whom we heard the oracles, the most knowing and inspired of all Celtica. But who are they possessed by now? What demons have come to light that fire? Why those cries?"

We heard hurrying steps behind us. We turned, and recognised Barynthus in the darkness.

"What's happening?" asked Merlin.

"Master," replied the old pilot, still out of breath from running, "two women from the convent came just now with torches to try to set fire to the *Keravel*. They didn't know I was aboard and spoke between themselves. Thus I learned that they'd been sent by Morgane, with orders to put her own vessel in a safe place to prevent us leaving the isle. When they saw me, they fled. But be careful Master, they want to cut your throat, you and your disciple."

"I know," said Merlin.

"Yes, but perhaps what you don't know is what I've just learned. Colombe has fallen into their hands and they're going to immolate her on the stone this very night, when the moon has risen."

These words struck me like a dagger through the heart. But the Master kept his head and gripped me firmly by the shoulders.

"Be calm, my son," he said. And I saw the fire in his eyes. "We are going to save Colombe."

"You," he added, turning to Barynthus, "run as quickly as you can to the *Keravel* to prevent another attack. Set sail immediately and come and wait for us behind the convent on the wild coast. I will sound the Korn-boud."

"As you say, Master," replied the pilot and disappeared into the night.

"And now," Merlin told me, "we must hurry! Run to the manor and find a sword. Bring my bow and arrows. But what we have to do is a difficult task. So when we have penetrated the sacred walls, obey me exactly, do nothing impulsive! All depends on you and your firmness. Let's go!"

The enclosed convent had walls that gave onto the high seas, and the brazier that now rose into the sky helped us to find our way through the rocks below the steep cliffs where Merlin knew a secret entrance giving onto the stones of sacrifice.

How can I describe the sight before our eyes, without my flesh quivering again, despite the years that have passed since that frightful memory?

In the red light of an immense pyre that the high priestess Morgane stoked with a torch, dishevelled women danced, splashed with blood, their strident cries mixed with the crackling of flames. And on the stone of the dolmen, where two furies tied her with ropes, lay Colombe, completely naked, her breasts slashed with frightful wounds, struggling under the stranglehold of Skléra, knife in hand, about to bleed her like a beast.

The confusion was such in that hellish orgy, that our appearance was not immediately noticed. Merlin profited from that with these rapid instructions: "Stand firm at the entrance to the underground passage and defend the access at all costs. Use the bow to hold the Sènes at bay. Shoot as many times as necessary. I will see to the rest!"

Then with prodigious agility he leaped toward Skléra, who had her back turned to him, totally concentrated on her atrocious work. With the point of his sword he struck her fiercely in the neck at the top of the spine. Skléra collapsed. Then he plunged his blade into the pyre and an oriflamme of blinding embers sprang out on the stupefied virgins.

As for me, I had released my arrows; a druidess fell, her throat transfixed. Merlin rapidly cut the bonds of the victim and seized the body of Colombe and came running back to the entrance of the passage.

"Dogs! Acursed!" cried Morgane, whose fury equalled her surprise, and leaping on the dolmen she threw her flaming torch at Merlin. She had wanted our defeat, but now she found her act was the cause of our victory. In fact Merlin protected himself from the arrival of the torch with his sword, and as the entrance to the secret corridor was covered with enormous bushes of dry gorse, these flared up at once, forming a curtain of flames that covered our retreat.

When we came out on the wild coast, a desolate otherworldly scene, the moon rose and bathed us in its cold light.

As I ran over the pebbles and slippery rocks behind the Master, who still carried his precious burden, hastening to the shore, I tried to see if Colombe was still alive. But Merlin had wrapped his cloak around her, and without turning, did not address a word to me.

Suddenly, in a gap in the cliffs, that showed before us in the lunar brightness, we saw the ship of the faithful Barynthus. Discovering that fragile craft swinging on the phosphorescent sea, our last chance to flee this cursed island, I felt there was no finer thing on earth than the accord of free beings deciding to meet at a perilous hour in an agreed place. And I saw this marine vision, so perfectly Breton, as an eternal symbol of freedom and escape.

"Take Colombe," Merlin said, "and follow me. I will go down to the shore and hail Barynthus."

I took the body of Colombe in my arms. She was unconscious, but still alive, for placing my ear to her young mutilated chest I could hear her heart still beating. I advanced, tottering on the pebbles and through the pools, and holding her naked body against me, trying to staunch the blood that ran from her wounds. I loved her, and she belonged to me. I would willingly have given her all my own heart's blood. I could say nothing, but felt such an intoxication, a mixture of pain and desire, that I was sure, despite my innocence, that no human creature in the most frenzied transports of the flesh could be so totally and gloriously possessed. I found myself on the beach without even knowing where I was.

Barynthus came to meet us in his dinghy. Merlin asked me to consign Colombe to him again. I embarked in my turn and heard the sound of the oars as in a dream.

Half an hour later we were at sea, under the sails of the *Keravel*, and could no longer distinguish the Isle of Séna other than the flames of the pyre that faded into the night.

VI

It was after that disastrous night that what I will call the Passion of my Master Merlin began. Was it because, to save Colombe, he had once more ceded to the temptation of violence and spilled blood? Or must we admit that, as the sequence of events will demonstrate, that the impassive sage of Celtica could not resist the prodigious radiance of Colombe, and felt painfully split between the beliefs of his fathers and the lights of the new religion? Anyhow, his supernatural will seemed to abandon him, giving place to a sort of fatalism, and he seemed more and more to give in to the powers of destiny.

Barynthus headed for the cape by the pole star as Merlin examined and summarily dressed the wounds of Colombe. These attentions tore a long moan from her that made me shudder. She came out of her torpor and ceased to complain, fixing on each of us her wide eyes, in which suffering had tarnished their brightness. Her body was horribly gashed, and she had lost much blood on the way from the convent to the *Keravel*. The Master placed his finger to her temple and looked at me with evident anxiety.

"My friends," murmured Colombe suddenly in a clear voice, "I know I'm going to die. It is the will of God, I feel it, and rejoice to think that my earthly trials are finally over."

"It is still in my power to save you," said Merlin, extending his hands over her.

But Colombe stiffened with a supreme effort. "In heaven's name," she cried, "spare me your enchantments. Understand me, Merlin my friend, I have immense respect for you, and I know you are pure among the pure. But if I die, it is to confess my faith. For I believe that the Lord Christ is much greater than you, and that it is to Him alone that I owe my health."

"But didn't your Christ himself thus perform a miracle?" asked Merlin.

"I have already placed my soul into his divine hands. May all be according to his will!"

At these words I fell to my knees before the couch, stifling my tears. Colombe gave me her hand that I covered with kisses.

"Adragante, my beloved," she murmured almost in a whisper, "don't be sad, for you are the only being down here to whom I would want to give my heart if I had been free to do so for an earthly love. And it is because I am going to die that I am permitted to tell you I love you. God does not forbid me to love, but it was perhaps necessary for you, the reborn, as for me, the disincarnate, that our love should be beyond the flesh, above the earth. Regret nothing. Don't be bitter. Nothing from now on can separate our two souls. I will meet you again above, where God will unite and reunite us, and when we will know such nuptial joys as will never end..."

As she spoke and revealed the secrets of her heart to me with such simplicity, it was as if I were immersed in an unknown light. No doubt I had only been resuscitated by Merlin to hear this confession of love, falling from the lips of a young agonised girl, that worked a spiritual transformation within me. I knew now that I possessed my viaticum, my last rites, and that it would accompany me until the hour of my death.

However, Colombe weakened and her breathing became irregular. "Now I want to speak to your Master," she gasped.

Merlin, who had heard, approached.

"Merlin, give me your hand and listen to me. I want to charge you with a mission when I am no more. Can I count on you?"

"Yes," replied Merlin.

"I don't know if you can bury me according to Christian law. But whatever becomes of me, when you reach land, go to the end of the Crozon peninsula and look for my brother Gueltaz. He is a Christian monk, a clearer of forests, and thus an enemy of your cult. But you have treated me with such generosity that I have faith in you, as in a father and, if I dared, I would even say one of us..."

The young girl stopped, lost for breath. I wiped the cold sweat from her brow.

"Drink," said Merlin, putting the pilot's flask to her lips.

While the Master moistened the young girl's tongue I thought of the woes of our human nature, from which we take our fleeting pleasures, but remain humiliated in its physical needs and all its forms including agony. In this bloodied body, overthrown, rested the same admirable creature who had appeared on the bridge of the *Keravel*. Her soul wanted to go. I saw it palpitating in her hollowed face, and at the corners of her mouth, tense with pain.

"Listen," said Colombe, in a voice so weak we had to lean over her to hear her last words… "Tell Gueltaz how I died, and let him know the place of my burial. Farewell my knights, my dear friends. I die in the faith of Christ, praying that he will enlighten you…"

She tried to make the sign of the cross and it was Merlin himself who guided her hand. Her lips moved for a last time, and I believe I heard her say "Amen".

I leaned over her, and putting my lips to hers, received her last breath.

Day broke sad and cold on the Iroise sea off Brittany. The lowering sky was an immensity of grey and the winds had veered to the west, driving us toward the coast.

All night we watched over the body of Colombe with the Master. His intention was to disembark at the grottoes of Morgat, to bury the young girl according to the wishes she had expressed, and try to meet the monk Gueltaz and let him know the circumstances of the tragic death of his young fellow worshipper.

We were occupied with sewing up Colombe's body in a piece of sail when we heard the voice of Barynthus:

"Merlin, come up to the bridge!"

I was about to follow the steps of the Mage when the voice of the pilot rang out again.

"Quick, help me put on sail. We're being pursued! Look!"

I climbed up to the windward side and looked under the sail, supposing it was a pirate, the scourge of the coasts. But the ship that I saw profiled on the waves about a thousand yards away did not have the serpent on its prow generally used by Vikings.

"It's the *Gwerzid*," said Merlin, "Morgane's ship. There are women on board with bows and arrows – the furies are on the tracks of the *Keravel*. It's going to be a battle to the death. We'll have to fight again."

"We can try to get to Morgat," said Barynthus.

"Impossible. Morgan's boat is faster than ours. We can only escape her by a trick… or some other way.

"What should we do about Colombe's body?"

"I don't know. We'll have to see. But its presence on board the *Keravel* obliges us to flee rather than engage in combat. Head to the north, the nearest reefs, and make for depths where the *Gwerzid*, of greater tonnage, won't be able to follow."

Barynthus was certainly unequalled as a navigator but in this circumstance could not evaluate the chances when it was a question of a mage against a faery.

This sea chase, which began before the point of Pen-Hir to end at nightfall before the Aber-Wrach river mouth, remains, with the death of Colombe, one of the most dramatic memories of my life.

Near the Causeway of the Black Rocks, Barynthus, tacking among the reefs of white water, successfully gained a greater distance from the ship of the sea amazons, but when we were free of the straits and arrived in view of the rocks of Portsall, the *Gwerzid* reappeared on the port side more menacing than ever, and two arrows, one of which grazed the pilot, struck into the mast of the *Keravel*.

As if in a dream, Merlin gazed at the horizon, and I heard him murmur, as if talking to himself: "For the first time in my life I have had to run from priestesses of whom I was the initiator and of whom I could have been the Pontiff! No doubt I could still exercise my power, and turn the elements against this boat of harpies, whose sails are filled only with the winds of hate. But the time of enchantments is passed. Since last night I have entered into my Saturn time. It is strange that this transit of my astral destiny should coincide with the death of Colombe. All becomes destined in my life. Now comes the time of a will greater than my own."

I looked at the Master in sad surprise. A furrow had crossed his brow and I read hesitation in his magnificent gaze.

"My Garden of Olives," he continued, "will not be at all like that of the Sage of the East. But I know it will come close to it. And those two arrows planted in the mast are signs for me."

As night fell the *Gwerzid* grew closer. I could distinguish the tall figure of Morgane on the prow. Suddenly I saw her take her bow, crying: "This one is for you, Merlin! Druid traitor!"

Then I, Adragante the Gaël, with the speed of light, pulled an arrow from the quiver of the mage, the only one, I thought, that could hurt a faery!

A piercing cry was the response to my act. Morgane, her hand pierced, dropped her bow into the sea.

"In all my life," said Merlin, "I have never seen a mortal wound a faery. It's true that since I resuscitated you at Salisbury you are not a mortal like the others. But I regret your act, for it drags you with me into the arena of evil spells."

After a while he continued. "But what after all does it matter that the faeries revenge themselves if we have Truth and Strength within us. And if we know how to die like that adorable young girl whose soul now awakes in the Infinite Light! It's about her, Adragante, or more exactly what remains of her, that we must now think. The *Gwerzid* prevents us from dropping anchor. We cannot dream of landing the remains of Colombe. So, my son, let us give her the last rites and confide her to the sea, where cradled in its waves, she will find her final rest."

The moment of great separation had arrived. Yet a strange peace filled my heart as we carried the sail that contained my beloved in its folds onto the bridge.

I indicated the starboard side, desiring to hide the ceremony from the eyes of the female crew of the *Gwerzid*.

"No," replied Merlin, "on the contrary, we must do it to port, between Morgane's ship and our own. An inner voice tells me that the body of the virgin who has been martyred by the Sènes will serve as a shield for us against them. May the God of Colombe grant us this proof of his power!"

Through the cloth that already concealed its form like a shroud, I piously embraced the body of the young girl. Then we carried her to the bulkhead where the Master laid his hands on her for the last time.

"Farewell Colombe," he said, "predestined child, daughter of the light, deliver yourself to the immensity, go to return to the Universe!"

We lowered her body to the water line, and having let her go, remained leaning over the waves that came to submerge her.

Then came the miracle.

The surface of the sea suddenly became phosphorescent, and the water opened to allow the passage of Colombe, who remained suspended above the waves in a halo of blinding light. She was dressed in her long religious robe and held before her mouth the index finger of her right hand as if to impose silence. Her eyes were wide open and fixed upon us. Then suddenly, her form melted into a cloud and she disappeared from our sight. But behind her, and rising to the sky, an enormous wall of fog protected us from the *Gwerzid* and allowed us to gain the open sea.

Colombe had saved us. All three of us were astounded witnesses of her apparition and the prodigy that accompanied it. God had granted the miracle!

An hour later the *Keravel* could reef her sails and drop anchor in a cove to the north west of Aber-Wrach.

VII

Among the events that I recall here, that form the end of my Celtic saga, some things occurred beyond my presence. I cannot however pass over them in silence, for they give some understanding of this mystic adventure and its enlightening epilogue.

Here then is what Barynthus and tradition have to tell of them, for when I saw Merlin again in Domnonée he was already the prey of the faery Viviane. And the rapid drama that followed soon after his return to the crystal dwelling gave him no time to tell me of the enchantments of the forest of Paimpont and the last secrets of the manor.

We remained some days at Aber-Wrach aboard the *Keravel,* when Merlin asked us to take to sea without him and return to Cézembre. It was there I lived all that winter, seeing Barynthus the Taciturn only at rare intervals, who in those first months left a few messages from the Master.

Through him I learned that Merlin had been able to find Gueltaz, Colombe's Christian companion, who ran a group of missionaries on the Crozon peninsular. He could then give this monk the message with which Colombe had charged him, and profit from that by discussing with him the penetration of the principles of the new religion into our beliefs and venerable traditions. They resulted principally in causing havoc in our forests, and their 'bishops' forbidding the population of Armorica from frequenting the sacred fountains or continuing their devotions to the trees and menhirs. In this conflict of religions he foresaw the fratricidal struggles and interminable convulsions in the establishment of future society.

At the end of winter, which was long and hard, Merlin ceased to send me his news. Barynthus knew only that the Mage had been invited by Viviane to Paimpont, not far from the magic fountain of Barenton, in a mysterious valley situated at the very heart of Broceliande where the faery possessed a manor that no traveller had ever dared approach.

Some have since claimed that Morgane, who could have joined Viviane, would have excited the jealousy of her former rival, by telling her of the adventure with Colombe, and persuading her that if the bard had risked so much to save her life, he must certainly have fallen in love with the Christian virgin.

Viviane, always taken with Merlin, thus resolved to attach herself to him in turn. The Enchanter had rejoined her at the first moon of Mars, and Viviane was adroit enough to glean from her friend the three occult words and three great secrets of the enchantment of love.

The first philtre, composed of nightshade and vervain, brought on a deep sleep and split the personality, returning it to almost a vegetable condition. This was followed by a Venusian pentacle, based on an astrological theme, drawn from the hair of the amorous woman and the dried blood of a dove. And finally the hawthorn enchantment, in which nine circles were traced with magic formulae, creating an impassable zone all round the beloved object.

And so it was that in the first days of Spring, when the forest, gorged with sap, prepared alcoves of love around the quietness of the lakes, and washed the leaves with the colours of Venus, Viviane, after her wheedling, recommenced the thousand year spell by inscribing round Merlin nine magic circles, making him a prisoner of his own spells.

What had happened to the heart of the mage? And why did this man of superior essence, who called himself 'saved', accept entering in full knowledge the trap laid for him by the enchantress? Was it to know all of the tests of the flesh? To end his condition as a man by submitting to all that remained in him of pride in the fatalities of passionate life?

We do not know. Whatever it was, he let it happen. What remains even more surprising would be if he, the Seer, did not know that this enchantment would lead to his downfall.

After having kept Merlin captive for many moons, Viviane, happy to have controlled his power, broke the enchantment of the hawthorn, with the idea to trying after that the power of the love philtre on her prisoner. Then both, having left Paimpont, returned to the crystal château during the last moon of Spring, a little after the annual fire festival. It was there that I saw them again.

The first evening, when I took Viviane's alezane mare to the stables the animal took a false step and hurt her fetlock so badly that she reared up with almost diabolic fury. I owed my safety to the arrival of Barynthus, the colossus of the sea, without whose intervention I would certainly have been trampled. When he had done all possible to quieten the mare and lead her to her stall she was gasping and covered with foam and we had great trouble in dressing the wound.

This accident seemed to me a bad augury. I had only just met Merlin again, who was happy to give me the accolade on his arrival, but without telling me, as had been his custom, the events of his life since our separation. I could not sleep that night, and went out many times to look towards the windows of the manor, whose lights, more agitated than usual, had something lugubrious about them.

During the next day I did not see either Merlin or Viviane. The château remained hermetically sealed under a torrid sun. Barynthus himself did not appear, and I wandered a long time on the beach before a marsh of stagnant water, prey to an insurmountable anxiety.

At nightfall when I returned to the lower house, I was brushed by the wing of a bird, feeling its breath on my neck, then I distinctly heard at intervals the funereal cry of a rook, nocturnal messenger of death.

I had hardly returned home when I threw myself on my bed, fully dressed, and went to sleep almost immediately. It was Barynthus who woke me. He was shaking me violently as if I were a drowned man, and saying: "What's happened? You've been asleep for two days! Two days and two nights! I've come several times to try and wake you. Serious things have been happening, very serious. Have you been enchanted too, like our Master Merlin?"

At these words, I gathered myself together and sat up.

"Yes, enchanted," continued Barynthus. "Bewitched by the faery, no doubt. He was sleeping like you for two days before the cavern of Cézembre. Perhaps you can wake him? Come with me to a clearing in the Wood of Love to see him. They'll say he's dead!"

Barynthus spoke truly. When we arrived at the clearing of Cézembre which gave out onto the sea, Merlin lay between two hawthorn bushes, his head resting on a velvet cushion taken from the château. His face and his crossed hands had the paleness of marble and not a breath seemed to move his chest.

I had never seen Merlin sleep. And nothing was more moving than to find myself for the first time in the presence of this kind of corpse. I reached out to touch it to try to awaken him. But no more than Barynthus could I cross the few steps that separated me from the body of my Master. An invisible wall stood between him and us.

"These are Viviane's enchantments" growled Barynthus. "The Master has drunk the love philtre. He is lost."

Such a thing seemed impossible, and I could not leave the Wood of Love without trying to save Merlin from this charm. I knew that a certain name contained magnetic force. I needed to call the Master, to make him return to the surface of the abyss. I made Barynthus understand that we must take this last chance to save our friend.

"Merlin! Merlin! Merlin!" cried the man of the sea in a powerful voice that echoed through the silence of the woods.

The mage did not budge. But the faery Viviane appeared before the hawthorn bush. She was dressed in a long golden robe and held a long hazel wand in her hand. Her auburn hair flowed to her shoulders, and in her hardened face lights shot from her green eyes.

"Go!" she cried, "or it will be the worse for you! The sleeping Merlin belongs to me. Never again will the mage of Celtica leave the frontiers of the holy forest. Never again will he evade the magic circle of my love!"

She had hardly said these words when a long whistling could be heard at the entrance of the cave of Cézembre. The sailor seized me brutally and turned me on my heels.

"Look!" he cried in a strangled voice.

And I began to tremble in my turn when I saw Gorsiff, the king of the serpents, who in rapid undulations swept toward the hawthorn bush where the faery stood.

"What do we do?" stammered Barynthus. "We're done for! I know only one in the whole world who can control the king of the serpents. You know him as well as I do. It's the Master. And the Master's bewitched. We can't do anything for him, and he can do nothing for us!"

Already the monster was upon us. In that moment of agony I called Colombe to help me. Was this the saint's reply? The terrible sound of Gorsiff's scales at my side that branched off suddenly and rushed at Viviane.

The faery, her eyes dilated in horror, raised her magic wand to try to halt the king of the serpents, but the moment of Ankou had arrived, the moment against which nothing can prevail. The thing that is there for all eternity, and needs must be so. There she already was, and no magic circle, no heavenly intervention could prevent the horrible consequence, last ring of fate of all the mysterious links of Destiny.

A terrified cry, supernaturally sharp, made the sky tremble and seemed to make the flame of the sun flicker. God in heaven! What an espousal! Viviane struggled, losing her breath in the embrace of the giant reptile entwined round her body.

The curls of her splendid hair shot out around her like flames, and in her revolted face her mouth opened wide. Gorsiff drew back his large flat head in which shone two golden eyes, and advancing his enormous jaws, plunged his fangs into the faery's tongue. Her whole glorious body shook in a last spasm. Then with the sound of a moan like a sacrificed dove, Viviane was dead!

"Dead!" cried Merlin, who awoke at the same moment, all her spells having been undone with the life of the seductress.

He had a frightful pallor, and tears shone in his clear eyes.

"Ossi! Ossa! Ossia!" he commanded in an imperious voice, extending his hands towards Gorsiff.

The monster dropped his prey and flattened to the ground. Merlin took the inert body of Viviane in his arms and said: "I do not have the right to curse you, Gorsiff, for you represent the strength of things down here, the all-powerful instinct, the divine irresponsibility of the elementals who give a check to human nature. But your reign ends with that of the faery of the forests, whose person should have remained sacred. By this crime you are yourself condemned to death. Go! Back!"

The serpent drew back its head making a strange hissing, then slid across the Wood of Love, and we saw it rushing to throw itself in the sea.

⁅⁆

Merlin had said it. The bite of the king of the serpents had no remedy. We left in the evening to bury Viviane in a secret place in Broceliande. The gnomes of Merlin had enclosed the faery in a crystal coffin, hermetically sealed and magnetised by the Master, where she would rest for ever, like a waxwork, preserved from decomposition.

At midnight when the moon was high in the sky, Merlin wanted to go down himself with the cords of the coffin of the enchantress to the hollow under the jet of water of the druid fountain. The faeries surrounded us during the burial: Nivona, Centaurée, Sanguine, Azilis, Limosela, Scabieuse, Osmonda, Lobélia, Belladone, led by Mona-la-Cendrée, the faery of the heathland and farewells.

The trees of the endless forest leaned their green plumes over us. Still and silent, the hosts of Broceliande gathered round the fountain. Thousands of birds wheeled in the moonlight, nightjars and rooks, swallows, lanceolate bats, and the nightingales themselves were silent

145

before the remains of the royal faery. The eyes of the screech and horned owls shone in the shadowed lines of the oak trees. From the bottom of the alleyways wild boars ran, accompanied by their sows and their young, along with the bronze furred bears who reared up suddenly on their hind legs. An immense stag, ancestor of the forest solitudes, led, with his head of ten horns, a procession of hinds with silvery fur, while a college of wolves widened out in an undulating circle around the silence of the mourning clearing.

The faeries threw branches of hawthorn into the fountain, and Merlin, having scattered the leaves of a tuft of gorse on the clear water, improvised this last farewell on Viviane's lyre:

Holy fountain and sacred stones
Mourn for the one who is no more
The god succumbed and the druid vanquished
The temple dead this night with the fay.

The deforesting monks are in Broceliande
The sap of the trees falls with dead wood
The axe has replaced our golden sickle
The gallop of Anku is in the land!

Eurydice of the North, for whom Orpheus
Went down to the hells to cross the threshold.
Celtica lies at the base of your coffin
And all the West dies in your faery lap.

Farewell Viviane, sleep in the zodiacal night
That the fountain may sing until the last day
And your faery blood pass in the lustral water
Where our children will come to baptise their loves!

Merlin finished his song with a sad arpeggio, responded to by an immense moan that was carried in the wind from the depths of the forests. The moon was suddenly veiled. And we were no more than shades beyond the shadows.

"Take this lyre, Adragante," the Master told me. "I give it to you in memory of us. The time for spells is over. The hour of sacrifice has come for me. I must now go on to cut my last notch in eternity. Farewell my son!"

He embraced me hard against him, and his lips touched my temples.

On Merlin's orders, Viviane's mare, whose wound had healed, had been brought by Barynthus. Without another word, Merlin mounted it, and I heard his last gallop fade and then vanish into the night.

Broken by grief, I sat on the fresh grass before the tomb of Viviane, where I lost no time in falling asleep.

When I awoke the clearing was deserted, under a sky of absolute blue. The murmurs of life passed through the brakes, and I felt the summer breeze on my face, carrying the pollen of the worlds. From the bottom of its mysterious tabernacle, a cuckoo called, messenger of the solstice.

Had I been dreaming? Alas no! For by leaning over the fountain I could see the crystal coffin, where the body of the faery seemed to move in the shimmering eddies of the jet of water whose droplets, forming rainbows in the sunlight, fell like ever fresh tears on her last sleep.

EPILOGUE

More than half a century has passed since that unforgettable night when Merlin the Mage of Britain left me, after having laid Viviane, the faery of Broceliande, in her tomb.

I have always lived in the lower house, near the rock crystal château, whose windows were blind from now on, haunted only by sea birds.

I hear the breaking sea far off, in its changing robe, and often go as far as the horn of Cézembre to commune with the infinite, in the midst of my seagull friends, who with their sharp clamour come to stand around me.

There one winter evening, long after the departure of the Master, I saw Barynthus again, who had been cruising with the *Keravel* off the shores of Scotland. He had made port of call at the Isle of Man in the Irish Sea, where he met various wandering druids, driven from their colleges in Cornwall by the Saxons or deprived of their living by Christian missionaries.

The old man of the sea always had his flask of hydromel with him and having been fishing brought a sea bass which he offered to share with me. I took him to my house and we roasted the fish over a fire of broom while the west wind that had risen with the sea blew over the dunes in violent gusts. Barynthus, who could thus not take to sea, passed the night on a seaweed mattress, and it was then I learned from him the presumed end of my master Merlin.

"To tell you the truth," he began, "no one knows exactly what happened to the Enchanter after he left us, or how he died. Is anyone sure, even, that he's dead? It's possible to doubt that with all the legends about him today. Aren't there some who claim that he wanted to be buried with Viviane? Others say that he has gone to find King Arthur, to sleep with him under the golden apple trees on the Isle of Avalon. While the fishermen of Cape Fréhal say they've seen him galloping on the promontory, the evening of the solstice fires. I think I once saw him myself, Adragante, sat on a rock, one stormy night, giving me a sign to luff to avoid a wreck. Have you seen him?"

At my negative response, Barynthus continued: "In that case, here's what I heard from the druids on the Isle of Man. They were serious well instructed men not in the habit of accepting fairy stories. But for them the death of Merlin seemed to be in no doubt."

I was overcome by these words from the pilot. He saw that and put his knotty salt bitten hand on my shoulder.

"It's a sad story," he continued, "but one difficult to believe, if one accepts what the druids say, that Merlin would be dead within twelve moons after the burial of Viviane, but it seems likely that after he left us our Master went to the Carnute tribe at one of our oldest sanctuaries, and then on to Lutèce, where he marked out the boundaries and then took part in the edification of a Temple dedicated to the Virgin Mary constructed at the end of the river island.* Would he really have done that? We shall probably never know, any more than we will know by what magical means our friend found himself soon after that in the land of Lanark, in Scotland, at the source of the Clyde. Merlin? Or the spirit of Merlin?

"There, it appears, that Morgane, who had never ceased to pursue him in her hatred, rediscovered his trail, thanks to the emissaries of Skléra, and ended by avenging herself, as only a faery knows how to do! She persuaded the shepherds of the Grampian mountains that Merlin had betrayed the religion of his ancestors, and assassinated Viviane. The thing seemed quite likely as the mage frequented again the Christian anchorites established in that region.

"Led on by Morgane, the shepherds watched the comings and goings of Merlin, and surprised him one evening at the edge of the river, where they stoned him. The druids add that Morgane and her druidesses took part in the crime, and cut up Merlin's body, that with his head they threw into the gulf of Corra Linn Fall."

At this tragic tale I found myself fainting. No possible doubt! Merlin was dead! I had that searing certainty by recalling the horrible premonitory vision that had appeared to me, at my initiation, in the obsidian mirror.

$$\div$$

Barynthus took to the sea towards noon. For the rest of the day, which was darkened by autumn clouds, I wandered in the dunes and on the strand, recalling all I could of the vanished Master, and the tears that flowed from my eyes mingled with the light rain and the salt wind. The only two beings, apart from Viviane, who had been the essence of my affective life on earth, were gone forever. Separated from the rest

---

* Site of Nôtre Dame cathedral on the Ile de la Cité, Paris.

of men by my infirmity, I found myself in unspeakable isolation, like the horizon that extended before me to a perspective of nothingness.

Night had fallen before I decided to return to the lower house. Now imagine my stupor, on approaching the threshold, to see the window brightly lit. It could not be the return of Barynthus, whose sail I had seen slowly receding until it disappeared over the far curve of the waves.

Who was it then?

With beating heart, I pressed on and pushed open the door.

It was Merlin! Standing before the hearth! Merlin alive! Dressed as before in the long, silk embroidered, linen robe, held at the waist by a leather belt, and wearing at his neck the golden torque of the bards, from which hung the pectoral five pointed star. Nothing had changed from his earthly appearance, apart from his gaze, that had a strange gentleness, and that his stature, which seemed overwhelming. He was surrounded by an intense light giving my room the brightness of full daylight.

And at the same time this light entered my heart.

I felt no fear, nor surprise, and at a sign from him, I sat on the stool, continuing to have my fill of his presence.

"Adragante, my son," he said, after a while, "I bring you peace."

I recognised his tone of voice, even though its resonance seemed supernatural.

He continued. "You see before you the image of the Saved. The bloody tests – now forgotten – through which I had to pass to come out of the circle of Abred are of little matter! One has to suffer to die; and die to be reborn to a higher life. No creature escapes that final passage. No man of flesh and blood can avoid crossing the dark strait that represents the fermentation of the shadows.

"It was necessary for the body of light in which you see me clad to be born in sorrow. All birth involves a sacrifice. But the events of time can no more have any effect upon it. I am a new born of the infinite light!

"I thus give thanks to the criminal hands that allowed me to accomplish my last transformation. Viviane dead made me see the Truth, but it was through my own death that I discovered the divine kingdom, from which nothing from now on can frustrate me. That, my child, is the great lesson of death. It is the great door by which we come out from transitory illusions to find eternal realities.

"No doubt, you, the resurrected of Salisbury, will wonder why you should have been restored by me to your perishable form, and have to confront the torments of death again. But I needed a witness to pass on my testament to the sons of Celtica. Thus your name will remain inseparable from mine, like the mistletoe that stays attached to the oak from which it receives its vegetal blood, just as I would not be able to live spiritually without receiving the sap of divine Power.

"But your death will be easy, for you have not bitten the fruits of the earth.

"It was otherwise for me. The Sublime Father, whose designs are not revealed to us, wanted my birth, my life and death, to form part of that line of redeemers who, over the centuries, have revealed a part of the divine message for successive generations. Mysterious similarities make us brothers of each other, and the blood of the gods flows in our veins, for, only our Mothers – may their bodies be blessed – participated in the earthly conception.

"To the four corners of the world, these few predestined must carry the weight of the universal sorrow, enlighten a handful of disciples, and put the seal on their work by the sacrifice of their life. In the saga of the human race, they represent the bloodied footbridge which *joins* earth to heaven. They are living emblems of the Supreme Being, who consents to immolate himself and divide his members throughout creation, until the day when all will be saved and gathered again into primordial Unity.

"Dionysus was torn apart by the Titans, but his heart, recovered by Minerva, shines in the disc of the sun. Osiris was cut in pieces by Typhon, but his body, reconstituted by Isis, reigns today in the invisible world. Krishna, the sage of India, died pierced by the arrows of the archers of Kansa, but his remains, cremated by his disciples, left the flames of the pyre in a figure of light. Finally the divine sage of Palestine, who died at Jerusalem from a torture reserved for criminals, is come from the tomb, a vanquisher of Caesar, imposing the lesson of charity and love upon the world.

"My role, one of the last to come, was to be a place of intersection between the old druidism and newly born christianity. To try to reconcile the two doctrines, without renouncing as much of the traditional beliefs of the ancestors. I was also of the race of the 'avendhyon' and poets, like Orpheus of Thrace, my brother from the South. And because, like him, I wanted to react against the bloody excesses of the feminine cult, I had to suffer too, the vengeance of my enemies.

"It remains for future Bretons to find my scattered members, that symbolise, like those of my predecessors, the dispersions and divisions menacing in the near future the purest races. For long, for very long, men will follow the paths of hatred and mutilation of each other before coming to understand that the Universe can only accomplish its redemption as a single soul in a single body.

"The God-Christ did not die on the cross to set believers one against the other and foment new carnage, but to proclaim the law of Love, that rests on two precepts, and apart from its rites, whose diversity will be only apparent, remain the prerogative of each sacerdotal authority.

"Finally, among the 'loving' who have chosen for their mission to pull all into their own furrow, when the hour of the final redemption sounds, some will have practised renunciation by turning their back on human nature; others have accepted drinking the cup of life to the dregs, in assuming all the risks of the earthly condition.

"I am of these last. I have received my punishment for it, for joy that can be a matrix for future sorrows. But pain itself is good and salutary, as our Mother Nature proves in giving us both life and death.

"Nearer to man than the Man-God, more visibly submitting to errors and divisions than he, I have spilled the blood of my brothers in battle, I have lowered myself by living completely in creaturely passions, and have abdicated the pride of the adept in the consummation of carnal love, where the central mystery of life is hidden.

"I have thus shown by my example that one can become a son of God without proscribing natural law, and that supreme humanity perhaps resides in the acceptance of the adventures of the blood, which we owe to our soul and all the promises attached to its being.

"You, my son, are at the other pole, and it is in *that* that the disciple will be greater than the Master in the balance of the Weigher of Souls. Even more, that you will live in obscurity, anonymous and alone like the bird of the sky who disappears without leaving a trace.

"The moment has come to leave you, but it is not goodbye between us. Any time you call me, you will feel my invisible presence. I will always be near to inspire and to sustain you.

"In the world to come, over which strange threats weigh, other sages will come to continue the work of salvation, and serve as a counter-balance to the immensity of bestiality and crime.

"But it is through Woman that the face of the Earth will be renewed. Morgane, Viviane, Colombe represent the evolution of three kingdoms, over which reigns the Virgin Mary, crowned with stars, whom I have seen in the city of Light, and who will return on the last day to save the living and the dead!"

Those were the last words of Merlin. I had fallen to my knees, while he laid his hands on me. It was like being dazzled by a redoubling of the light. Then, suddenly, all was gone.

My heart raised by a supernatural force, I passed the rest of the night meditating in the shadows.

And now I am here.

My task is over. Old and full of years, I am seated before my clay lamp, with my seagull pen useless from now on, with nothing left to do on earth but wait for death.

The dawn rises on a dismal December day. It has been snowing for some days, and through the window of the lower house I can see the abandoned crystal manor, through a forest of thistles and nettles, buried in a mountain of gorse.

The trees of Broceliande fall one after the other to the axe of the monks, as if giving witness to the out flowing of my life. At the druid fountain, where the jet of water has been silent for many days, the body of Viviane rests, but I have not seen the faeries again.

Barynthus died at sea many long years ago. Colombe sometimes comes to visit me in dream.

It is of her that I ceaselessly think. She, my promise of eternal nights, and like Merlin, my beloved Master, the immortal commander of Celtica.

Death stands behind the door, I know, and soon I will rise to be delivered in the ether, where both will receive me in their arms.

God, give me your Strength – and in that Strength the courage to suffer – to suffer for Truth – and in the Truth all light – and to find in my light – Life, Fire, Truth – the true, the beautiful and the divine. Amen!

www.ingramcontent.com/pod-product-compliance
Lightning Source LLC
Chambersburg PA
CBHW030335020726
47493CB00004B/1286